"I WANT YOU MORE THAN ANYTHING!"

"Katherine, Katherine." He repeated her name again and again, moving his lips up over her cheek and into her hair.

His hand was on her shoulder and gliding powerfully downward, pulling her closer into his embrace. Shivers of delight followed the pressure of his fingers as his hand dipped dangerously over her hip. Katherine threw aside any pretense of resistance and in glorious abandon lifted her face in search of his lips. They were there, eager and waiting, and when they came together, a fire burst within her, filling every vein with wild desire.

CANDLELIGHT ECSTASY ROMANCES™

STRICTLY BUSINESS

Gloria Renwick

A CANDLELIGHT ECSTASY ROMANCE™

Published by
Dell Publishing Co., Inc.
1 Dag Hammarskjold Plaza
New York, New York 10017

Dell ® TM 681510, Dell Publishing Co., Inc.

Candlelight Ecstasy Romance™ is a trademark of
Dell Publishing Co., Inc., New York, New York.

ISBN: 0-440-17727-8

Printed in the United States of America
First printing—July 1982

Dear Reader:

In response to your continued enthusiasm for Candlelight Ecstasy Romances™, we are increasing the number of new titles from four to six per month.

We are delighted to present sensuous novels set in America, depicting modern American men and women as they confront the provocative problems of modern relationships.

Throughout the history of the Candlelight line, Dell has tried to maintain a high standard of excellence, to give you the finest in reading enjoyment. That is now and will remain our most ardent ambition.

Anne Gisonny
Editor
Candlelight Romances

CHAPTER ONE

"Good morning, Miss Graham," Katherine Dunn, with unaccustomed timidity, greeted Butler's chief publicist. Katherine was in the second week of this, the best job opportunity to come her way, and had not yet dared to be less than formal with her infamous boss.

"It's too hot to be good," Eleanor rasped, referring to the classic Los Angeles October heat wave while patting her damp forehead.

Katherine watched as the older woman went through her daily "first things" routine. Eleanor scanned her desktop, looking for the smallest item out of place. Next came the proprietary examination of each drawer, as though she expected something to be missing. The same scrutiny was given the white-on-white office that was the seat of Eleanor Graham's power. At last she rose from her desk and with solid, uncompromising steps moved to the wall where every detail of present and future promotions was plotted.

She was small, this epitome of female success, square and compact. Her almost white hair was neat but plain.

The same could be said for her clothes. For almost forty years she had been the brains behind Butler's famous ads without ever permitting a shred of their glamor and elegance to rub off on her.

I never thought of it before, but she's a real martinet, Katherine thought. A successful one too, considering how Eleanor had helped to mastermind Butler's metamorphosis from a beautiful, but provincial, outpost on Wilshire Boulevard to the mecca of American fashion.

Eleanor was staring at the day's calendar.

"Have you checked the foyer mannequins yet?" she asked, her voice already accusing.

"Er . . . no . . . I—I just got in myself," Katherine stammered. It was a full hour before the store opened. There was plenty of time to check all of the display changes. Why did this woman persist in treating her as though she were worthlessly lazy instead of hardworking and competent as Katherine knew herself to be?

Eleanor turned from the board, her face tight with anger.

"What are you doing standing there, girl? Get to it!" The shrill words bounced off the walls.

Katherine paled and clenched her fists. She was both mortified and resentful, yet she could say nothing. Any employer would be more desirable, but this was the job she wanted. Without a word she obeyed.

Upon reaching the great foyer and seeing the trio of stately mannequins so artfully posed there, Katherine had to admit there was reason for Eleanor's obsessive insistence on display checks.

"Look at that!" she spoke aloud. "I told Willy to use the handbags from today's ad and he picked up last week's leftovers!"

Finding actual work to do eased Katherine's tension: for a few minutes, at least, she could forget about her differences with Eleanor. She looked at the famous Art Deco clock that shared the three-story entry wall with the founder's portrait, and was grateful to see how much time was left before the doors opened and floods of the wealthy and the curious filled the aisles.

Quickly Katherine assembled the correct merchandise, and just as quickly she stepped into the exotic grouping, looking, for an instant, as though she were part of it. Tall, reed-slim, with alabaster skin and flaming copper-penny hair, Katherine had all it took to be a high-fashion model —until a closer look revealed a nose too long and a mouth too wide. No, Katherine's looks were too "individual" for big-money modeling, a dozen agencies had told her.

Katherine had accepted this bitter end to dreams of quick success with the quiet fortitude that had helped her past previous disappointments. Using credits from two years of junior college, she had plunged into NYU's marketing program and graduated with honors and a reputation for predicting trends. Even then she had found that the available jobs were exceedingly limited and the pay was even worse. Looking for brighter prospects, Katherine had followed the sun to California, but while her experience and reputation grew, the opportunity she sought continued to elude her.

There were times when she had almost quit, shut the door on her one-room apartment and gone back to the small lumber town she had come from. But the bleak prospect of living a life like her mother's had always been enough to stop her. That, too, was why she had resisted the proposals that had come her way. The ruins of her parents' marriage had been so scarring that she had sealed off her emotions in self-defense.

Not that Katherine did not want love; she did. The sight of couples lost in their own special magic never failed to turn her heart with a twist of envy. Yet her fears remained, and as a consequence Katherine had dedicated her quick mind and abundant energy to the business of fashion, giving to it the passion she might have given a lover.

At last, two weeks earlier, the golden chance had finally come. It was not a sure thing by any means, but at least it was a toehold. Katherine smiled as she thought of her job title, Assistant to the Assistant Publicist. On the other hand, she knew that to be assistant anything was something when you worked at Butler's. This was the company that in sixty years had worked its way up to dominate American retail fashion, and it was Katherine's private conviction that if the management was as sharp as it should be, then the next sixty years were assured too.

Even now, as she carefully replaced the guilty handbags, Katherine could barely believe that luck had come at last.

Dear Dee, she thought. *A friend in deed, and heaven knows I needed her.* It had been Dee Cummings, another "failed" model, who had called Katherine with the offer.

"Listen, sweetie," Dee had said in her usual light-bright style. "Put on your best suit and polish up your pumps because have I got a job offer for you!" Dee had gone on to explain that she was soon to take a maternity leave and the assistant publicist's job would be up for grabs. Katherine had been grateful, but after all it was just a temporary job, wasn't it?

"No! No, Katherine" came the emphatic response. "Now that Peter's out of med school and practicing at last, I'm retiring from active duty. Oh, I might do some part-time work at Butler's branch in Pacifica, but when this little bundle beneath my belt arrives, I'm becoming a homebody."

Katherine's hopes had soared. The assistant publicist's spot at Butler's was the highest-paying, most desirable position of its sort in the business. And everyone knew that the boss, Eleanor Graham, was within five years of retirement. It was also known that her reputation for being difficult to work for was the reason why the pay was so good. Nonetheless there must have been dozens of people clamoring for this chance. Yes, Dee agreed, there were. But if Katherine played her cards right and came in to assist Dee for the next two months, it would be Katherine who would have the inside chance at actually getting it. So, with no more security than that, Katherine Dunn had quit her year-old job with a sportswear manufacturer and come to Butler's.

The first week had been enough to tell her that not only was it going to be difficult winning the assistant's position but job security would be nonexistent. Eleanor Graham was the toughest of taskmasters. Even when she knew you were working hard, she cracked a mean whip of words. It was her trademark, Dee had said, and the only way she showed her approval was by *not* firing you. Well, Eleanor had not fired her yet and it was Tuesday of week number two. So far she had held on.

Katherine adjusted the third handbag, a snappy little three-hundred-dollar snakeskin clutch, snugly beneath the mannequin's arm. The soft luxury of the model's heather wool Valentino suit caused Katherine to take an involuntary deep breath.

"Someday I'm going to wear clothes like this," she promised herself, and then glanced at her own let's-pretend silk blouse and plain brown skirt. Not that anything was wrong with them; she had been happy enough to buy them wholesale from her previous employer. But after five years in the business she knew quality by sight. She knew it by smell and touch too. What was more, she had learned that price tags did not always tell the real story. Some "name" designers were known to occasionally slip inferior quality into the market, and because of their high-fashion labels the merchandise would sell, returning incredible profits. More than once the undiscerning public had come to believe that the sleazy look was "in." Valentino, on the other hand, was a certainty, always first class. Chanel too. Katherine gave a minor collar adjustment to a silk tweed suit jacket from the house of the famous little Coco and began to weave herself backward out of the now impeccable tableau.

Katherine stepped out of the setting. She stood poised, the three offending handbags over her left arm, right hand on hip. Her concentration was complete, so much so, that even though the corner of her eye saw Eleanor Graham and an exceedingly tall man coming directly toward her, Katherine's mind did not see them.

Intently she gave a final study to the mannequin figures and to the opulent backdrop beyond: the soaring black marble walls, the tourmaline-green beneath her feet, the glass cases edged with gilt and filled with a king's ransom of merchandise.

"Ah," Katherine murmured, "perfect." She took one more backward step and struck something that threw her totally off balance and careening to the floor with such force that in the future the next few seconds would be forever blurred.

Fuzzily she tried to focus on the man who stood directly above her. Somehow, her mind told her, she must have stepped into him; that would explain the fall.

Katherine, who was tall herself, recognized the man as a giant, standing a good eight inches beyond her own five foot eleven. She also recognized that his appearance was familiar: the thick and wavy black-brown hair, the strong and forceful jawline, the long and narrow eyes beneath a straight line of brow.

It was the eyes that held her, hynotically, like a small animal trapped in its predator's gaze. The eyes were

12

smoldering with unreadable meaning, and instinctively Katherine knew that the dark of their depths would, if she would let them, lead her into passages and chambers where she had never been before.

The imminent danger that his eyes suggested jolted her from the shock of the fall and led her attention from the threat of the man to Eleanor, who was standing at his side.

Oh, no! Katherine's thoughts cried out in silent horror. *Please, this can't be true!*

Color flushed her face as she imagined the picture she created, sprawled upon the floor with her slim skirt—her new skirt—ripped to the hip, runs in her nylons, and a sore ankle. How awful it was to be absolutely helpless, to know that fate had just twisted the course of your life, and to be unable to do a single thing about it. This and more ran through her mind as she felt the rigid dislike in Eleanor Graham's gaze.

"My, what a novel way to introduce a new—a temporary—employee," Eleanor was saying, her voice cold and piercing as an icy stiletto. "This is Dee's idea of a replacement." Eleanor gestured toward Katherine as though the latter were an inanimate object. "Not that I have ever thought much of Dee's ideas," she continued, "but this one seems to be particularly poor. The only talent she has so far displayed is that of tripping over her own feet."

"I disagree with you, Eleanor," the man said. His voice, deep and resonant, held just a hint of amusement. "I see quite a lot of obvious talent." Now those dark and frightening eyes were skimming Katherine's body, and she knew that not a line or curve had been overlooked.

"Red hair and long shapely stems, hmm?" He smiled, showing strong white teeth against a deeply tanned complexion.

Katherine bit back tears of pain and humiliation. Vainly

13

she tried to grapple with the long tear in her skirt while at the same time attempting to stand. Both efforts failed as her Scottish temper and color rose.

The giant's smile grew broader. "Our American Beauty seems to have a few thorns." In one sweeping motion he bent down to Katherine. "You really shouldn't try to walk, you know." He lifted her into his arms as if she were a feather. "At least not until we can check for possible damage."

Katherine protested loudly and did her best to squirm free. "Put me down! I can take care of myself!"

"Don't you find it nice to have a little help now and then?" His voice was mild and reasonable and had the predictable effect of making Katherine all the more belligerent.

"No!" she cried defiantly into the ear three inches away.

"Well"—his eyes turned upon her and brought her to instant silence—"you're getting it whether you like it or not!

"Sorry to leave you with the pickup, Eleanor," he said, referring to the scattered handbags, "but I'm taking our friend here into your office. I think one of her ankles is beginning to swell."

Behind them Eleanor's voice could be heard, speaking caustically about lawsuits and release forms, before its acid tones were mercifully swallowed by the deep inner space of Butler's high vaulted chambers.

Katherine was fairly certain of the identity of this man who had so forthrightly picked her up—as though she belonged to him. But pride determined she would not speak his name until he ventured it himself. She had ceased resisting, partially because she knew it was useless and partially because her ankle did hurt and she was uncertain as to how well she could walk alone. Most of all she was determined not to risk making a fool of herself a second time.

The man continued to stride in long effortless steps, his footfalls echoing down the empty aisles: past cosmetics, where the scent of a thousand flowers always bloomed; past jewelry; and into the cushioned inner sanctum of the executive offices.

Katherine studied his profile in silence, resenting him and everything about him with an anger that went beyond reason and carried her back into the darker memories of her childhood.

The last man who had carried her like this was her father. He, too, had lifted her with the confident assurance of possession, that wonderful, joyful, redheaded Scotsman she had loved so much and who, she had been so certain, loved her beyond all measure. He had been her adored ideal, her Prince Charming who would save her from every evil. He was her own, her father.

It had been a summer day that last time, and Jimmy Dunn had taken his wife and nine-year-old daughter up to the dam. Katherine would forever remember he had not been quite so gay that day. Still, he had rented a little boat and taken them for a sail. Later, when dusk was falling and she was so very tired, he had carried her just like this. She had snuggled her head into the crook of his neck and he had crooned a Scottish tune to his Kathy, his Katherine, his Kate. All day, for his pale young wife, he had been full of tender kisses. Yet that night, sometime in the dreadful abyss of darkness, he had left without a word, without a note, without a sound. They had never seen him again.

Why? Why? The questions were never answered satisfactorily. Debts? Yes, but not anything overwhelming. Another woman? Maybe. A waitress from the roadside café had disappeared the same night. Katherine and her mother had learned to manage, not well, but above poverty level—just above.

Katherine did not like to think about these things; yet, unwanted and uninvited, they returned to show her just how vulnerable she really was.

Maybe it was an old emotional scar, as Dee said. But then Dee had never been abandoned by the one she loved and trusted most. When her father had left, and for years thereafter, Katherine had been convinced it had been her fault, that she did not deserve his love. Gradually she had overcome this burden of imagined guilt and rebuilt her self-respect. Her mother had not been so fortunate.

Sarah Dunn's disappointment had grown into a festering bitterness that ultimately incorporated all men into the sins of Jimmy. How many times had she said, "Never trust a man, Katherine, they just want one thing." Later, when the boys began to call she said, "Don't you go gettin' lovey-dovey with any man, Katherine. There's not one of 'em who wasn't born bad where women are concerned." Even at the end, when the years of anger and privation had burnt her out and she lay dying, Sarah could not forgive. "Katherine, baby," she had whispered, "go build yourself a good life and don't let any man in—ever!"

Now whenever Katherine thought of her parents it was with heavy sadness. Together they had made sure there could be no tender Kathy, no loving Kate, only Katherine —proud, distant, and alone.

The man holding her now turned his head and caught her staring at him. What he read in her expression she could not guess, but he smiled and started to speak. Abruptly she turned her head and thrust out her chin in a self-conscious attempt at disdain.

"Well, my pretty package, I'm glad to see we've reached our destination."

16

He walked through Eleanor's office door and over to her white chenille couch.

"For all your looks you're not much fun, you know."

"I don't mean to be," Katherine hissed between her teeth.

"Ah-ha! A bit of flame to go with the red hair. Good enough." Carefully he settled her into the cushions and looked down. "If those green eyes of yours carried weapons, I'd be dead, but since they don't, I'll risk it." Using the same possessive manner that had already triggered her emotions, the man proceeded to examine Katherine's ankles, then her lower legs, then her knees.

As with everything else concerning him, his hands were strong and sure. They were handsome and sensual too, with long supple fingers crowning the broad palms. The touch of the skin was slightly rough, belying any thought that these hands were unaccustomed to real work. Grooming, however, was like the rest of the man— meticulous, with the soft feathering of fine black hair on the backs and closely trimmed nails gleaming like ten pink pearls in contrast to the weathered skin.

Seconds passed. Katherine found herself speechless in the wake of this stranger's takeover of her body. Clearly he was an expert. The way in which he was manipulating her bones and joints was entirely professional. So too was the line of his attention. No matter his earlier remarks, there was nothing flirtatious here. Katherine's respect grew. Whether she had been two or eighty-two, this man's interest would have been the same. Just one odd piece did not fit the puzzle, and she had been so sure that she had recognized him from the portrait.

"Are you a doctor?" she asked, genuinely curious.

"No." His answer was matter-of-fact and it served the purpose of solving her little mystery.

Katherine waited for him to say more. When he did not,

she realized that his concentration was such that whether she spoke or not he would not notice. This was the moment to demand his attention with a score of cutting remarks, but Katherine found her temper was gone. It was impossible to be angry with someone who was doing his best to be of help.

"Truce?" Her voice wavered just the tiniest bit, but it was enough to erase her cold reserve and admit at least a thimbleful of her vulnerability.

He looked up. She was smiling. It was a small smile, tight and rather rigid, but it was a smile nonetheless. His response was immediate and cut a wide white crescent across the lower half of his face.

Katherine's breath caught in her throat. If he had been attractive before, he was disarmingly so now. She would have to be careful.

"Truce?" He answered with the same question. "Sure. But I didn't know there was a war."

She decided to ignore the latter half of his response. After all, if he was who she thought he might be, she could not afford to alienate him. Still, she was not sure.

"If you're not a doctor, how do you know so much about—" She had almost used the word *anatomy* but found it suddenly sounded too personal. "About bones and . . . things." The "things" was added rather weakly.

"Oooh, ouch!" She winced. He had taken hold of her left foot and was slowly rotating it about the ankle.

"Sorry, but really you can count yourself lucky. The swelling is minor and it looks like a small sprain involving just a portion of the top of your foot. Here, see?"

She looked down beneath his hand.

"You don't seem to have any back complaints, do you?" She nodded negatively. "Good. Just favor your left foot for a day or two and you'll be like new."

Gently he released her foot. "And to answer your ques-

18

tion," he continued, "I got my medical know-how in Nam." He paused. It was obvious that Vietnam was not the best of memories.

"I learned a whole lot of things over there." His voice turned flat and hard and his eyes looked to a far distance. There was a heavy silence. Then, with a clear display of self-discipline, he pulled himself to the present, his focus telescoping back until it rested fully on Katherine.

"Say"—the brightness in his voice was only slightly brittle—"with dimensions like yours what are you doing here behind the lights when you should be out in front of them?"

"I tried." Now it was Katherine's turn to have her voice go tight. She always hated discussing her failure. Yet this man had revealed a corner of himself to her and she knew, with one of those rare insights into the future, that it was vitally important for her to reciprocate.

"It was this," she went on, gesturing to her face, "that did me in."

He rocked back on his heels, crossed his arms over his chest, and surveyed her critically. At last he shook his head.

"I still don't understand." He looked and sounded so earnest, she could not help but laugh.

"My nose and mouth," she said, finding it amazing that she could laugh at such a hurt. "They're too 'individual.' "

She could see he had missed her meaning.

"Look." She started to explain and at once her business manner came to the fore. "A good photographer's model can't have a nose or a mouth or eyes—well, eyes are not quite so bad—that people are going to remember from picture to picture. If they do, if they remember the model, then they are forgetting to look at the merchandise, and that's the model's job—to sell fashion, not herself."

19

As her manner changed, so did his. Now he was sarcastic and offensively forward.

"Hmmm. A woman who looks like you"—again his eyes raked her from head to toe—"could sell me on anything." Deliberately he had dragged out the last three syllables. The effort was not wasted on Katherine. She bristled visibly. He smiled. It seemed to please him that she was irritated.

"Yes, with your long, slim stems and red plumage you are quite the pluckable rose, aren't you? 'A rose by any other name . . .'" He paused, his eyes still mocking her. "By the way, what's your name?"

"Katherine Dunn," she responded with icy formality.

"Katherine, huh? Why not Kathy or Kate?" His tone was brittle and contemptuous. "Why do all of you career women have to be so damnably officious? Why can't you be a success and a warm human being too?"

The gall of the man. How dare he think he could be familiar with her! Kathy or Kate! He had no right!

Katherine's mind was filled with silent fury, but her voice was cool and deadly calm.

"And why do you modern men feel so threatened, so emasculated, that you have to resort to such petty pompousness. Standing there pointing your finger at me. Demanding my name." She paused. It was her turn to eye him from head to toe: his massive physique, his careful grooming, his custom-tailored suit, his handmade Italian shoes. She did it slowly and with freezing objectivity. At last she asked the question she had been wanting to ask all along. "Well, who are you?"

Katherine knew all too well how her appearance was compromising her efforts to hold her own in this war of words. It was difficult, if not impossible, to look businesslike when lying prone on a couch with your feet elevated and your skirt ripped.

20

Her adversary, his temper gone, could not resist the humor of the moment. He drew himself to his full six foot seven inches, squared his shoulders, tucked his chin, and answered respectfully.

"Chad Adam Butler. At your service, miss."

Adding a broad wink, he stepped out of Eleanor's office and disappeared down the hall, leaving Katherine sputtering with rage. She gritted her teeth in an effort to regain her calm and asked herself why. Why did this man have this ridiculous effect upon her? Why had she let her temper go, something she had long before learned to contain, when this was a person she had needed to impress favorably? Yes, she had known who he was. It had not been hard to guess. He was the physical reincarnation of the other Chad: his grandfather, Chadwick Butler, the founder of this fabulous chain, whose portrait hung above the entry of this, his original creation.

A frown creased her smooth brow. Had she, with her silly burst of temper, blown away her best career chance—the one she had worked so hard to obtain?

She sat up and swung her legs around so that she could put on the shoes Chad Butler had tossed on the carpet. The left foot did hurt a bit, but he had been right. The swelling was barely noticeable and she had been lucky. A broken ankle or even a bad sprain would have kept her from work and finished her chances at Butler's. Despondently she rested her head upon a hand. If she had not finished herself, she thought. After all, Chad Butler had not been the one in the wrong. He had actually acted in an old-fashioned, gallant way. It was she who had chosen to react to him as if he were a Cro-Magnon dragging her to his cave. He could not know that he had touched a raw nerve from her childhood, and even if he had made a few forward remarks, her attitude was still inexcusable. Maybe that was just his manner. Maybe he had been trying to gloss over her embarrassment, trying to make her feel more relaxed and at ease in a difficult situation.

Katherine felt a hot blush in her cheeks as she relived the last twenty minutes. The events of the morning, which had started out so surely, had led her to a position where, by her own error, she had given up a part of that which she cherished above all things—total control of her own destiny. She knew, with a chilling certainty, that in one instant—when she had taken that last backward step—fate had walked in and altered her life. Her future at Butler's was bound to be affected, and that would determine everything.

Would Eleanor Graham walk through that door and say "You're fired"? Or would a call come from Chad Butler's office bearing the same blunt message? Katherine, for the first time in her life, realized just how vulnerable each person is to the actions and attitudes of others, forcing a mutual dependency she had sought to avoid. It was the first crack in her wall of aloof self-reliance.

Whatever happened she was not going to be caught like this. She forced her thoughts back to matters at hand and was in the act of dialing Alterations to ask for assistance when Dee Cummings burst into the office.

Dee was shorter than Katherine by a significant three inches. Her round brown eyes, pixie nose, and perennially short haircut had typecast her as an "ingenue" model when she and Katherine met. They had simultaneously discovered their assignment lists were shrinking, Katherine's because of her "individual" face, and Dee's because at twenty-four she had already exceeded the ingenue age limit by two years. There had been one all-night cry session when they both decided to try fashion promotion and when their friendship had been sealed by three boxes of soggy tissues and two bottles of cheap wine.

Through some miracle, as Dee would always claim, she

had landed the Butler's position and a handsome medical student in quick order. Katherine, on the other hand, had struggled from dead-end job to dead-end job and lived a monastic life, which Dee very vocally considered both wasteful and boring. Now she was in her eighth month of pregnancy and considered nothing more desirable than husband, baby, hearth, and home. She wanted Katherine to inherit her job, but even more she wanted her dearest friend to know the same inner glow of happiness that she had discovered. As a result, no matter Katherine's disinterest, Dee resolutely sought potential husbands for her friend. This morning she had been given new reason for hope.

"Katherine, tell me!" Dee bubbled excitedly. "What's been going on? I just met Chad out in the hall and wow, did you make an impression on him!"

Katherine gestured Dee to silence while she completed making arrangements with one of the alteration ladies to come down to Publicity and fetch her skirt. Dee could barely conceal her curiosity and fidgeted restlessly until Katherine finished.

"Yes, Dee, I know the impression I made." Katherine spoke without emotion. "The kind that will probably cost me whatever chance I had at getting your job." Quietly, in an almost expressionless voice, Katherine told the story.

Dee listened intently, her brown eyes glistening with interest. When Katherine finished, after making a final comment on how badly she had botched her meeting with the boss's son, Dee eagerly contradicted on two points.

"First, dear Katherine, Chad is more than the boss's son. He is the boss. Adam Butler retired in August."

Katherine's mood dropped still lower. This could make the incident even more detrimental to her ambitions.

"And as far as the impression you made," Dee went on

blithely as though the whole horrid scene had been a triumph, "I can tell when a man is interested, and Chad Butler is interested in you."

Katherine shook her head emphatically. Her attitude toward men always annoyed Dee.

"Listen, Katherine, I know I'm right. There he was, walking along the hall, right out there." She pointed toward the office door. "He had this big smile on his face, and you know how gorgeous he is when he smiles—melts even my loyal heart. And when he saw me, he stopped and said, 'Say, Dee, your friend Katherine Dunn is quite a girl. I'm glad you brought her here.' Now how's that for a positive reaction?"

Katherine brightened. "I hope you're right. This job means everything to me."

"For pity's sake, Katherine!" Dee's voice was filled with disgust. "When you have a handsome, charming, fabulously rich man interested in you, who cares about a job?"

"I do, and you know why."

Her friend sighed deeply. "Maybe your father was a louse, but that doesn't mean all men are bad. Give it a chance. You don't know what you're missing."

"You're my friend, Dee, and I love you dearly, but please, once and for all, understand. I think marriage and a family are just great for you, but not for me. I don't want any part of them. This"—her gesture encompassed Eleanor Graham's office—"is what I want."

"And at sixty to be just like Eleanor, old and empty and cross as a bear? No, Katherine. You have too much love to give. Someday the right man is going to open up that closed-door heart of yours and you're going to be glad when he does."

Katherine sighed. It would be nice to believe there really was a Mr. Right searching just for her and all she had to do was stand still and wait until he came (and of course he would find her because in fairy tales the prince always finds the fair maiden). Then a thousand trumpets would blare, a new constellation would light the sky, and they would cruise off in a shiny Rolls to live blissfully together forever and ever. So nice to believe, but that plot belonged to Andersen or the Brothers Grimm or somebody. It certainly did not belong to her.

She turned to the rear of the office where a corridor led to another smaller and less grand office, which she and Dee shared: "We'd better get to work before Eleanor comes."

It was too late. The chief publicist had just entered and the fire in her eyes shot sparks at both Dee and Katherine.

"What are you two doing?" she demanded and then answered herself. "Nothing! Absolutely nothing. Well, let's see about that." Her tone had turned poisonous. "You, Dee, get up to Art and see how far they've gotten on the weekend ad layouts."

Dee sent Katherine a frightened look and scurried out of the doorway.

"As for you, Miss Dunn"—Eleanor always hissed her name—"get that copy finished. I want it by noon."

Gratefully Katherine fled to her desk. The old dragon might be breathing fire but there had been no talk of being fired, and that, in its way, was a victory.

The morning was busy. There was Eleanor's ad copy plus a stack of business correspondence and several phone messages that demanded response. Katherine paused only to slip into a workroom smock. She hoped that Alterations could mend her tattered skirt, but the lady who came for it was quite discouraging.

At eleven fifty a garment bag was delivered. The tag identified it as being from Designer Boutique. Katherine was mystified. No ad was scheduled for that department. Puzzled, she pulled the zipper. Inside hung an amber cashmere skirt. The Fortuni crest was emblazoned on the buckle and a business card was carefully pinned to the waist.

Katherine removed the card. It bore Chad Butler's name and a brief message on the back scrawled in a bold hand.

> *To make amends.*
> C.B.

Amazed and confused by possible ramifications of accepting this gift, Katherine did not hear Eleanor Graham enter until the older woman was at her elbow.

"Let me see that." Eleanor grabbed the card from Katherine's hand and examined it. "I thought I recognized Chad's writing. Make amends? For what? Not for your clumsiness surely. No." Her eyes narrowed as she regarded Katherine. "There must be something else. Something I don't know about . . . yet."

Katherine deeply resented the insinuation, yet there was nothing she could do but try to ignore it.

Eleanor moved to Katherine's desk and read over the completed copy. Finishing, she gave a quick nod of approval and returned the papers to their folder.

"Send this up to Art," she ordered. "Have them set the headings in thirty-eight point. That ought to be large enough to catch people's attention." Eleanor started down the corridor, changed her mind, and, turning on her heel, eyed Katherine narrowly.

"Miss Dunn," she hissed the name again. "You're new, but you'll soon hear of Chad's reputation. Don't flatter yourself. You're nothing special. Just another toy to amuse him—for a little while." Eleanor curled the edges of her mouth into a cruel half smile and walked away, leaving Katherine rosy with anger and frustration.

Soon the phone rang in the outer office and Katherine heard Eleanor's voice responding. From the sound of it, whatever Eleanor was being told she did not like.

The phone slammed back into its cradle and Eleanor's steps thundered down the corridor.

"You're a faster worker than I thought," she sneered at Katherine. "That was Chad's secretary. He wants you to attend the planning session this afternoon. It's a very important meeting. The Board of Directors will be there as well as every store manager and major department head." The contempt in her voice was growing. "They are all going to be wondering how you, a nobody, managed an invitation." Eleanor's eyes leered.

"They don't need to guess—do they, Miss Dunn?— with Chad there is only one way."

CHAPTER TWO

Twenty minutes later Katherine stepped off the elevator at the seventh floor and entered the Employees' Dining Room. It was a large sunny area decorated with only slightly less opulence than the public areas of the store.

Dee waved from across the room and gestured to the empty chair beside her.

"Katherine," she called, "bring me a chocolate pudding, will you?"

Nodding agreement, Katherine picked up a tray and moved into the cafeteria line. Her face was taut and grim, and her pulse still sounded loudly in her head as Eleanor Graham's horrid insinuations stubbornly echoed in her mind.

It was not that Katherine was any babe in the woods. She had received a number of "offers." Offers that would have made her life a great deal more luxurious: free trips, free meals, free clothes—one man even offered a free apartment. Katherine, however, had too much self-confidence and self-respect to sell herself. What was more, she refused to believe that the only means to success was acceptance of such ruthless dominance by men.

The smells of good food reminded her that she was hungry, and grateful for something more immediate to think about, Katherine turned her attention to the tempting array of choices. Everything looked so good, it was difficult to make a selection, except that in Katherine's case there was a budget that made the choice easy and always the same.

"Country vegetable and a cup of coffee, please," she said to the young girl behind the soup tureen.

"Any dessert?" the girl asked as she handed the order across the counter.

"Yes, the chocolate pudding." Katherine pointed to the line of prefilled dessert dishes waiting in a refrigerated cupboard.

"And how about a nice big slice of pie?" A now-familiar tanned hand placed a pie plate on her tray, and Katherine felt the strength of Chad Butler's arm pressing against her own.

A flood of color rushed madly into her cheeks. The cafeteria line was not that crowded. There was no need for him to stand so close, and yet she herself felt reluctant to move away. The moment seemed to hang in time, and she wanted to hold on and savor it. Vaguely she was aware of the young waitress holding out the dish of chocolate pudding, while Chad's penetrating gaze was turning her legs to tallow. It seemed an eternity before she could speak.

"No, thank you. I—" Katherine turned her wide-open and luminous green eyes up to meet Chad's. "I don't want it." But her eyes were saying other things in a manner that allowed Chad to drink in their meaning at his pleasure.

The young waitress had grown restless. "Do you want this, miss, or not?" The chocolate pudding wavered on its doilied plate. "Sorry, Mr. Butler," she continued with proper meekness, "but other people are waiting."

The mood shattered into a thousand glittering fragments and Katherine made a dreamy effort to catch a few for quiet reflection. Exchanging plates with the waitress, she found Chad to be persistently determined about her dietary choices.

"Really, Katherine," he called her name while once again setting the pie plate on her tray with his right hand and at the same time placing his left hand on her shoulder in a pleasant, friendly sort of gesture.

"Butler's Dutch apple is better even than Mom's and much better than that chocolate goo. Besides, I'd like to see you put more meat on those pretty bones of yours." He allowed his hand to glide down Katherine's back and come to rest just below her waist. The friendly touch had changed into something significantly different.

"Say, that skirt I picked out really does fit you like a glove." His hand shifted once more. "A very smooth glove."

Chad's familiarity hit Katherine like a stinging slap. She twisted away from his touch, feeling cheapened and disgusted. The meaning of Eleanor's ugly remarks became crystal clear and filled with truth or—if Katherine was not very careful—potential truth. Her eyes returned to Chad's face, but this time all the warmth and openness were gone, as though Katherine had slammed a heavy door upon her feelings.

"Keep your hands off of me, Mr. Butler." Katherine kept her voice intentionally soft so that no one else, not even the man with Chad, could hear. "I may be your employee, but I am not one of your—your toys!"

Chad smiled broadly and Katherine turned on her heel, making her way quickly through the cashier's line and walking in brisk, hard steps to Dee's table while a dozen pairs of eyes watched her stately progress with far more than a grain of curiosity.

"You've done it now," Dee announced happily as Katherine presented her with the much-maligned pudding. "In fifteen minutes all of Butler's will be buzzing about your flirtation with the boss—and half of the buzzers will be purple, green, and chartreuse with jealousy."

"It's not my flirtation!" Katherine's voice rose with anger, and the three little ladies from Hosiery who were sitting at the next table rose as one and eyed her with strong disapproval before they departed. Katherine ignored them and went on. "I didn't do anything. It was all him!"

"I know, I know, dear." Dee patted her hand solicitously and motioned for Katherine to sit down. "I saw the whole thing, even read your lips most of the time." Dee cocked her head like an adorable bright-eyed bird. "There's no more pretending that Chad Butler isn't interested in you as a woman," she said and smiled with smug satisfaction.

Katherine was having a hard time dealing with her temper. Dee's gloating smile was too much, and not wanting to say something unforgivable to her best friend, Katherine closed her eyes, turned her head, and took several deep relaxing breaths. When at last she reopened her eyes, it was to find herself once again face to face with Chad Butler and his companion. They had replaced the three ladies from Hosiery. There were a number of empty tables scattered about, but Chad had picked this one and no one in the room could doubt his reason.

He smiled at Katherine engagingly and tipped an imaginary hat with an elaborate gesture. His companion, a man of similar age and type but considerably smaller dimensions, looked at Katherine with friendly curiosity.

Katherine turned, saw she could receive no support

31

from Dee, who was struggling to overcome a paroxysm of giggles, and plunged into her soup as though she were searching for a life preserver.

"All right, Katherine, I promise not to say another word. At least not until I finish my dessert."

Katherine's eyes slid across the table and for the first time noted that there were two other pudding dishes sitting in front of Dee. Suddenly her sense of humor overcame her. Throwing back her thick, lustrous mane of red curls, she arched her slender white neck and laughed until her breath was gone.

Dee was offended. "Really, Katherine, it isn't anything that unusual. I just like Butler's pudding. . . ." Her voice trailed off and she joined her friend in gales of laughter.

"Oh, all right, I admit I've lost control," Dee gasped at last. "But I can't seem to help myself. I have this wild craving." And at that they both started laughing all over again.

At last, when they were quietly sipping their coffee, Katherine confided her worried reaction to earlier events, ending with Eleanor's insulting remark, which had been compounded by the actions of Chad Butler himself.

Dee had listened intently, and when Katherine finished, she picked up her spoon and stirred her coffee, staring into the steaming cup without finding an answer. Finally she shrugged her shoulders and looked at her friend sympathetically.

"I don't know what to tell you, Katherine, except that Eleanor is the price of the job, but I've said that before. She's notorious. And as long as she's a vice-president and voting member of the Board of Directors, and as long as Adam Butler's loyalty remains the same, well, everybody just has to put up with old Eleanor and her rotten disposition."

"But, Dee," Katherine asked in a lowered voice after

catching a glimpse of Chad's table and finding him engrossed in conversation with his male companion and a stunning Chinese girl who had just joined them, "how can a company such as Butler's afford to put up with someone like Eleanor who makes working conditions so difficult?"

"She hasn't always been this way," Dee answered. "In fact she was really rather nice when I started. It's just been the past year or so that she's undergone this change. And you know, Katherine, in her day Eleanor Graham was a genius. She saved Butler's from bankruptcy during World War Two, or at least that's what Adam Butler says. That's why he's so loyal to her.

"As far as Chad is concerned . . ." Dee indulged herself in a sidelong glance at Chad's table, and to Katherine's chagrin her eyebrows shot skyward at the sight of the beautiful young Chinese. "Well"—Dee turned back to Katherine and shrugged again—"there's no use denying he has a certain reputation."

"Do you mean that what Eleanor implied is really true?" Katherine demanded, her knuckles whitening in their grip about her cup.

Dee fidgeted with discomfort and avoided Katherine's gaze.

"I don't know exactly how true," she said and then, finding new courage, looked directly at her friend. "Besides, what if they are true? Is that so awfully bad? Even you have to admit that Chad is, in every way, most attractive."

"Then why hasn't he found some nice appropriate society princess and married her?" Katherine demanded with a certain amount of bitterness. "After all, he's got to be, what, in his midthirties? It's long since time he presented Butler's with another safe generation."

Dee regarded Katherine with surprise. "I don't know. There's lots of gossip, of course. The old-timers say it has

33

to do with an accident that killed Mrs. Butler and Chad's twin brother. They say that ever since, both men have made the business their family."

Katherine was horrified. "What a terrible thing! How did it happen?"

Dee shook her neat, dark head. "No one's ever said. All I know is that it happened years ago, when Chad and his brother were in college."

Katherine examined her hands, ashamed at her jealous outburst.

"Goes to show that everyone has their troubles, doesn't it? Here I am feeling sorry for myself because all I can afford for lunch is soup and crackers. By the way"—she gestured at the newly emptied pudding dish—"that cost thirty-five cents."

Dee groped in her purse and, upon extracting the proper change, plunked it noisily in front of Katherine. "Don't worry. When I'm gone, you'll have a paycheck big enough for beefsteak. But what then?"

"Why, the sky's the limit, Dee." Katherine spoke earnestly. "The person in your job is noticed by every big ad agency in America. And, if I can hang on long enough, Eleanor will retire and I'll be the one to fill her shoes."

Dee studied her friend carefully, as though she were seeing something brand new.

"You stagger me," she said at last, with more caution in her voice than Katherine was accustomed to hearing. "I've always known you were hardworking and ambitious, but this—"

"Why not?" Katherine interjected defensively. She did not like the way Dee was making her feel. "If I have the ability, why shouldn't I have the prize?"

"Isn't there some old saying about cold cash making a cold bed?"

34

Katherine's expression tightened and a guarded veil fell over her eyes.

Dee saw the symptoms but went on anyway. "Take the advice of someone who has a nice warm someone to snuggle up to. It's a much better way to live."

Katherine disregarded Dee's suggestion with a toss of the head. "Emotional entanglements are just what I don't need or want."

She was not going to let her friend know just how provocative she found Chad's attentions. How easy it would be to fall for him, to drop all defenses and allow him to make love to her. The very thought made her quiver; but that was something she could not allow to happen.

Katherine sipped her coffee and allowed her glance to drift, unseen beneath lowered lashes, to Chad's table. That girl across from him was beautiful with her wide, gentle eyes and cascade of raven hair falling over her shoulder as she bent forward over the table. And Chad? His face, as he leaned to meet her, was undeniably filled with excitement. A stabbing pain sliced through Katherine's body and she started to choke on the coffee.

"Are you all right?" Dee asked.

"Fine. Just fine," Katherine managed to respond as she brushed a tear from her eye. But she wasn't fine at all. She was dangerously attracted to a man who, if he could, would simply make her one more addition to his endless string of women, as Eleanor had so unpleasantly suggested.

She would have to watch herself. Chad was practiced enough to make sure his snares were soft and tempting. Katherine touched the skirt and was reminded that accepting gifts would be the first step. Too bad the price of self-respect was so high.

Dee was watching her with curiosity. Katherine could tell that her friend was trying to guess her thoughts.

"This skirt . . ." she blurted suddenly, caressing the soft cashmere. "Back it goes!"

"Back it goes? What are you talking about? I've been waiting for you to tell me where it came from."

Katherine nodded her head in Chad's direction. "Our generous boss sent it over 'to make amends,' as he put it, for causing my brown skirt to be ruined. But I'm not going to keep it. Just borrow it until after the meeting is over— then back it goes."

"What meeting?" Dee exclaimed in surprise.

Too late Katherine remembered that Dee would not have been invited. Frantically she sought to minimize the meeting's importance, but Dee knew better.

"You mean the Board of Directors' meeting this afternoon, don't you!" Dee's eyes flashed. "Who invited you? Certainly not Eleanor." Dee read Katherine's expression easily. "It was Chad, wasn't it?" The triumph in her voice rang clear. "See, Katherine, you do mean something special to him. I've been here three years and this kind of thing has never happened before." She paused and added soberly, "No wonder Eleanor is after you."

The scraping of nearby chairs diverted their attention. Chad and his party had risen and were readying to leave. As the others moved toward the doorway, Chad stepped to Katherine's side. His expression, as he looked down upon her, held a special warmth.

"You did receive my invitation to this afternoon's meeting?" His deep voice was soft as velvet.

Katherine was about to answer when Chad reached out and touched her cheek, sending a chill coursing down her spine.

"Say, Dee," he said, without moving his eyes from Katherine's face, "I've been checking our Miss Dunn's records. They're very impressive. I think I should make good use of her, don't you agree?" He did not wait for an answer but walked away, moving with the lithe grace of an athlete between the tables and over to the couple who waited at the door. Behind him he had left a delighted Dee and a limp, bewildered Katherine.

The meeting, as Eleanor had indicated, was going to be large. So large in fact that the board room had been ruled out and instead the famous underground theater had been assigned the honor of location.

Katherine was careful to arrive first. Much as she distrusted Eleanor Graham, she did not doubt the truth of the older woman's remark that Katherine's presence at the meeting would arouse curiosity. Katherine wondered too. Why had Chad made such a point of including her? Was it really, as he had said, because he found her background impressive and had found some way to utilize it? Or did he plan to utilize her in a different way—lead her up the proverbial garden path and then tell her that any permanent job would involve extracurricular activity? Games like that were played in business; it was a fact of life and Katherine knew it.

Katherine had just settled into a seat at the rear of the theater when someone in the projection booth flipped a switch and more than a score of crystal sconces illuminated the black marble walls, spreading their beams upward to reflect off the gold-leafed ceiling. A motor whirred softly and Katherine watched, fascinated, as the gold-banded black velvet curtains slipped open and a viewing screen slowly descended from above the stage.

Soon the room began to fill. Appropriately it was Chad and his party who arrived first. Katherine watched him and thought again of the game he might be playing. Could she resist? He was like a young Zeus, standing at the theater door greeting each arrival, and there was the power of thunderbolts in his hands. She knew. She had felt

37

his touch. Others had too, she reminded herself as Chad's luncheon companions moved to take their seats—but not before the girl had lifted her flowerlike face to whisper into Chad's ear. Again their familiarity struck at Katherine painfully, and she challenged herself to keep her thoughts off him and concentrate upon the roster of Butler's executives who were filing through the door. The Board of Directors was easy to spot. The only woman in their midst was Eleanor Graham, and the male members hovered about her as though she were a queen bee.

At last Chad stepped to the microphone and called the meeting to order. The immediate hush was an impressive tribute to his leadership. Using his abundant charm, Chad made a few introductory remarks, and Katherine noted how completely he held his people's attention. There could be no doubting that they would follow him anywhere.

Like all true leaders Chad had too much respect for his people's time to waste it. Quickly he reached the purpose of the meeting.

"You will recall"—his voice, strong and persuasive, filled the air—"that at our last meeting I recommended that Butler's develop a continuing series of signature designs, such as Givenchy, Dior, and a score of others have already done. These designs are like walking advertisements for those whose names appear on them."

Chad sidestepped the microphone and gestured appealingly to his audience.

"Let's face it, in an era of ever-escalating costs this type of self-promotion is absolute genius. So, the question has been"—he returned to the mike—"how do we go about doing it? How do we develop designs that will promote our name while still maintaining our insistence on first quality?" He paused for just an instant, then added, "I found the answer."

A murmur of excitement rippled through the audience. Chad lifted a hand and everyone was quiet. "And I found the answer in China."

Now the excitement was electric and Chad allowed the eager whispers to continue while he signalled up to the projectionist.

"With the help of some slides," he said, and again everyone was quiet, "and Karen Su-Chan, the most recent recipient of our annual Designer Award, I'm going to show you what Butler's will soon have all America talking about."

During the next several minutes, along with Chad's narration, Katherine and the rest of the audience were treated to an array of pictures of Chad's travels. There were Chad and others of his business delegation dressed in business suits and greeting Chinese government officials; Chad, in shirt-sleeves, walking the Great Wall; touring Ming tombs; visiting silk factories, oyster beds, and even a jade dealer. Chad, still in shirt-sleeves, mingling with his hosts: shaking hands, patting backs, asking questions, and all the time towering over even the tallest Chinese.

Katherine was becoming confused when suddenly there appeared a series of the same Chinese girl who had so recently been whispering into Chad's ear.

"You remember these gowns," Chad was telling them. "These are the designs that won Karen Su the award."

Then, as growing awareness filled the audience, Chad returned them, by way of the slides, to the silk factory, the oyster beds, and the jade merchant. Only now in each picture Karen Su-Chan and a smiling young man, introduced as her husband, appeared. Karen Su taking her three basic gowns and draping them in vivid swirls of silk damask that had been emblazoned with Butler's logo "B." Karen Su gazing into baskets of seed pears as she sketched

39

intricate ropes, bracelets, chokers and brooches. Karen Su looking on as an expert craftsman cut a rainbow of jade into a variety of the famous "B's."

Chad's idea was emerging and it was brilliant. These first Butler signature designs were to be a spectrum of softly draped caftans, which, by their opulent simplicity, were the perfect backdrop for a fortune in pearls and jade.

Katherine, along with everyone else, was left breathless. The promotion would be a sensation. The fact that this Karen Su-Chan was safely married and that her association with Chad was clearly business proved to be more of a relief to Katherine than she had any logical reason to expect.

The audience was applauding loudly, and when the clapping had begun to subside, voices could be heard throughout the theater, eagerly discussing the tie-ins for other departments: Home Furnishings, Men's Apparel, and even Children's Wear.

Chad gestured them to silence. "I thought you'd like it," he said with a straight face and brought the house down with laughter.

"Like it, we *love* it," someone cried out.

Chad answered them with a wide grin. "That's the kind of enthusiasm that's going to make this promotion the financial success I knew it could be. Keep it up!" His eyes swept the room and rested for just a second upon Katherine before he went on. "The timing on this is tight and we're going to need all of the talent we've got. That means full cooperation from the elevator operators to the president's office. Now, are there any questions?"

A few hands went up, and as Chad answered each one, Katherine was silently cheering him. His presentation had been masterful, and his calm, assured manner of command had won her confidence just as it had long since won the confidence of all the others.

The meeting was adjourned, and as the crowd filed out past Chad, Katherine noticed that each person was stopping to offer him their congratulations. Soon it would be her turn. What would she say? Quickly a half dozen appropriate phrases came to her, but none of them prepared her for what was to happen.

She approached Chad with a smile and a hand outstretched for a congratulatory handshake, but as she drew near him Chad reached out and grabbed her by the wrist, holding her fast in an iron grip.

"Stay here," he whispered urgently. "There're some people I want you to meet."

Before Katherine could gather her wits, Chad was introducing her to members of the Board of Directors.

"Yes," he told them, "this is Eleanor's newest bright light. Miss Dunn has already made quite a name for herself in our business and I'm counting on her talents for this new promotion."

Katherine's heart skipped a beat, as his words put to rest the doubts that had been troubling her. She looked over to where Eleanor Graham was standing. The older woman's expression was anything but friendly.

Chad's hold of Katherine's arm did not lessen. She could feel each of his fingers imprinting itself into her flesh. Finally the theater was almost empty, and Chad called to Eleanor and the man who had been his luncheon companion.

"This is Joe Parkman," he said to Katherine. "Joe is our ad agency man, the one who buys all of our media space."

Joe smiled. "It's a pleasure to meet you, Miss Dunn," he drawled. "And I hope you don't mind if I say that it's been a long time since I've had the chance to work with anyone so pretty."

Chad looked at Joe as though he disapproved. "That sounds nice, Joe, but Katherine doesn't need flattery and neither do I. What we do need is a lot of hard work." Turning to Eleanor, he went on. "I want you, Katherine, and Joe to fly up to Cielo tomorrow. Without the interruptions of the office we should get all of the basic planning done."

Eleanor did not look pleased. "Frankly, Chad, the quiet of your ranch makes me nervous, but," she sighed, "if that's what you want.

"By the way," she added, giving Katherine a quick glance, "wouldn't it be nice if it was explained to Miss Dunn why she would be wise to wear a dependable pair of walking shoes? You see," she said, turning to Katherine, "Chad values his privacy to a rather unique degree. There are absolutely no roads into or out of Casa del Cielo."

Katherine was stunned. She had heard about Chad's fly-in ranch but she had no idea it was as remote as this.

"Don't worry," Chad assured her. "The copter's never failed yet." He noticed the marks his fingers had left on her wrist. "Sorry," he said offhandedly, "I didn't know you were so tender."

Katherine was dismayed and somewhat hurt by this sudden change in his attitude. It seemed that as the business day waned, Chad's thoughts moved elsewhere and he could not leave their company quickly enough.

I wonder what her name is, Katherine thought bitterly.

The four of them emerged from the theater together, then Chad turned toward the executive parking lot, taking Joe with him. Katherine watched him walk away. He had not even bothered to say good night.

Eleanor smiled cynically. "You see, Miss Dunn? It's as I said—you're nothing special."

CHAPTER THREE

The alarm rang early but Katherine was already in the shower. She had found sleep impossible. Her turbulent thoughts had not allowed her to rest. Round and round they had swirled repeatedly, drawing the dark, rugged features of Chad Butler's face until his image was so deeply etched into her mind that it presented a constant disturbing picture whether her eyes were opened or closed. There was, however, one alarming difference. Each time she closed her eyes, Katherine not only saw Chad's face but she could feel his nearness too—his warm breath; his strong, sensual hands—and a raw ache filled her.

Never had a man had such an unnerving effect upon her, and in self-defense Katherine had fallen back to what for years had been the only interest of her life: the fashion business. Long before dawn she was sitting beneath the warming glow of a table lamp studying the most recent fashion publications and forcing herself to concentrate on Chad's Chinese venture and how she could contribute to its success. Yet no matter how hard she tried, the magnetic appeal of the man's incredible virility would not leave her alone and Katherine felt both excitement and fear.

She turned the shower water from hot to cold and shuddered as the icy pellets caused her white shoulders and firm breasts to tingle beneath their barrage. Outside the shower the tiny room was filled with steam. Katherine reached to push open the window. Instantly the hot dryness from beyond swept in, devouring every drop of moisture. It was going to be another scorching day and Katherine planned her clothes accordingly. What did one wear to a fly-in ranch anyway? Eleanor's advice about walking shoes came to mind. They were going to be so busy working on this new promotion that there could be no time for walking. A light dress and cool sandals, that would be the sensible choice.

Katherine stepped out of her bath into her all-purpose living room-bedroom-kitchenette. Her quarters might be small but she was rather proud of how cheery and attractive she had made them appear. Nonetheless she wrinkled her nose at the general mustiness of the air. The ventilation was terrible and during a heat wave—well! Katherine plugged in her little fan and flipped the switch. Thank God for modern devices. Maybe, if she really could secure the Butler's job, a better apartment was in the near future. Smiling at the possibility, she slipped into a flattering pale yellow linen that bore her embroidered monogram at its simple neckline. Checking the hot plate, she found her coffee and boiled egg simmering nicely.

A few quick strokes of the brush and her hair was properly tamed. Watching her reflection, Katherine reached out to touch the glowing strands that an errant ray of sun had set afire. She was glad that her coloring was so vivid that only a touch of artifice was needed to set it off. Even in her modeling days she had resented the time that making-up properly demanded.

Katherine glanced at her watch. Not much time remained before she had to leave. After finishing breakfast, she started to put the remnants of the night's reading back into order. *Vogue, Bazaar, L'Officiel, Town & Country.* Katherine nodded at each cover because from each one a familiar face smiled back. Jessica Spencer was featured on *Vogue,* Molly Highsmith on *Bazaar,* and Carole Seeley on both *L'Officiel* and *Town & Country.* Katherine returned the smiles of Jessica and Molly. She liked them both and enjoyed the hen parties they had whenever the other two were in town on assignment. Carole Seeley was another matter.

Carole was cruel, selfish, shallow, and vain; yet she looked like an angel turned movie star—if angels ever did such things. Katherine had privately entertained the thought that perhaps Carole really was an angel—from the other place, of course! It was impossible to forget how craftily Carole had gone about eliminating any possible competition. She had proved herself to be a no-holds-barred opponent five years before when they had all been new faces struggling to make a connection with a big-time Manhattan modeling agency. Carole had not hesitated to undermine the chances of her contemporaries by spreading her own poisonous brand of derogatory hints, innuendos, outright lies, and withering blasts of sarcasm. Katherine knew firsthand what it was like to be victimized by Carole and that made it all the more galling to see the golden-haired she-devil enjoying such international success.

Katherine's watch warned she was running late. *Damn the creature,* she thought as she shoved Carole Seeley's smiling face to the bottom of the magazine stack. *She's never caused me anything but trouble!*

Swiftly she gathered up her handbag and scurried out the door, muttering in frustration at the necessity of fussing with the door lock, which was as difficult to shut as it was to open.

Twenty minutes later the Wilshire bus let her out in front of Butler's and a quick elevator ride brought her to the seventh floor heliport a full four minutes before the assigned hour.

As she swung open the doors that led onto the rooftop, Katherine was genuinely surprised. She had never realized how utilitarian a rooftop could be, nor had she considered how large an area the roof of Butler's seventh floor could provide. Above soared Butler's smaller intermediate level and beyond that, looking from Katherine's viewpoint as though it led to the clouds, was the tapering pinnacle. Altogether the three-tiered silhouette was one of the most famous architectural designs of America's Art Deco period. Katherine's attention was still focused skyward when a sound from behind startled her.

"Good morning," a deep voice called, and she whirled to see Chad walking out from the store. Katherine had felt her heart take an unwanted leap at the first sound of his voice, and now she found that the sight of him was leaving her speechless.

Today, dressed in Western boots, jeans, and a cotton work shirt open almost to the waist, Chad was a far cry from the impeccably tailored businessman of yesterday. Yet his towering size and assertive maleness were even more apparent, and as he strode toward her in wide and easy steps, his white teeth flashed in a crooked grin and his dark eyes pulled at her magnetically.

"Sleep well?" His eyes twinkled teasingly. "I didn't. There was this redhead with terrific legs who kept invading my dreams. Know who I mean?"

Katherine blushed at his suggestion. "Where do you keep the helicopter?" she asked nervously, turning her head to avoid his uncomfortable penetrating gaze.

46

Chad laughed at her obvious discomfort. "Just you give me one welcoming smile and I'll deliver the chopper to your pretty feet."

Katherine tried to resist, but she could feel the power of his will pulling at her, making her submit to his commands just as surely as if he were a master puppeteer and she were one of his dolls.

Chad touched a forefinger to her lips. "You do that quite nicely, Katherine Dunn." His tone was still teasing. "A little practice and it might even become a habit."

He continued to watch her closely, and when she tried to move from the embarrassing familiarity that was so patently obvious in his expression, Chad caught her face in his hand and held her motionless. Katherine shivered and twisted free. What was he trying to do? Prove that he could handle her any way he liked, any time he wanted? Anger flushed her cheeks, but as she started to speak, Chad interrupted her with a rumble of laughter.

"All right, all right. Just calm down, I can take the hint."

He took her by the arm and guided her to one of the rooftop's few shaded areas.

"Wait here," he told her, his white teeth flashing in another broad smile. "I'll be back in a minute."

Katherine watched him walk across the blacktop and disappear into a shed. Soon the building's wide doors were sliding open and where moments before there had been only quiet inactivity suddenly a half dozen men were running purposefully about and the sound of a powerful engine could be heard. Katherine frowned slightly and thought of Chad the master puppeteer pulling everyone's strings, determining everyone's actions.

Moments later the red and gold helicopter was directly in front of her, just as Chad had promised. But where was he?

47

One of the men who had been running alongside the copter swung open the cockpit door and gestured for her to get in. Behind the flight controls she could see Chad, a radio set on his head and dark goggles covering his eyes.

"Climb in," he yelled above the incredible din of the motor.

Katherine obeyed and the door shut behind her. Following Chad's directions, she fastened her safety belt, noticing as she did the four empty seats behind them. Katherine looked out the window expecting to see Eleanor and the agency man, Joe Parkman, but they still had not arrived.

"All set?" Chad hollered.

Katherine nodded absently, still wondering why the others were so late. Suddenly the helicopter moved forward, and before she knew what was happening, Katherine saw the ground dropping away from them.

"Where are the others?" she cried.

"What?" Chad asked innocently.

"What happened to Eleanor and Joe?"

Chad was busy talking to the ground control and did not seem to hear her. At last, when they had gained more altitude, the sound of the giant propeller lessened a degree and Katherine restated her question a third time.

"Oh, them," Chad responded casually and glanced across at her. Even through the goggles Katherine could read the earthy danger in his eyes and the twist of his lips made the message a certainty. "Well, it's like this: I figure you and I can get more—ah—taken care of if those two aren't around."

For a moment Katherine was too stunned to speak, then she began to sputter. "You mean I'm going up there to this Casa del . . . Casa del—"

"Cielo. Casa del Cielo," Chad offered helpfully.

"Casa del Cielo. I'm going up there just with you? We're going to be *alone?*"

"Um-hmm." Chad nodded and reached over to give Katherine's knee a playful pat. "Just you and me, honey. 'A jug of wine, a loaf of bread, and thou.'"

"That's ridiculous!" Katherine cried indignantly while slapping at the offending hand. "Keep your hands to yourself and take me back this instant!" The mere suggestion that she might be spending time alone with this man was enough to give Katherine a severe fright.

She kept her eyes on Chad, waiting for him to turn the helicopter back, but he was occupied talking into his microphone, and all she could do was sit helplessly and fume. Seconds passed and Chad made no move to change their course.

"Are you or aren't you going to take me back?" she demanded.

"No" was the cheerful response.

"No, what?"

"No, I'm not going to take you back."

"But—but—but—" Katherine stammered in helpless fury.

"Consider yourself kidnapped, my sweet." Chad turned to her for a moment, and lifting one hand from the controls, he shoved the goggles back on his head and offered Katherine a slow, deliberate, mocking wink. "You might even find that you enjoy it."

"Oh!" Katherine was outraged. She whirled in her seat and stared blindly out through the glass. Her head was dizzy with questions. What did he have in mind? What "more" were they going to take care of? Nervously she looked at her hands. They were trembling with fright, and it was not just Chad that she feared. She was going to have to watch herself too. This man had a way about him that made her feel almost like a wanton. The palms of her

49

hands were moist and she forced herself to resist an urge to wipe them dry on the lap of her dress. She would be all right. Men had maneuvered her into tight places and she had always maneuvered herself right back out. The important thing was to retain her composure. She needed to be absolutely calm. Biting her lip as if to reinforce her determination, Katherine looked down and began an intent study of the panorama below.

Casa del Cielo. Katherine recalled the intriguing Spanish name of their destination. Dee had told her something of the place, though only Eleanor from the store had ever been there. It was supposed to be some sort of early California ranch, whose name meant "House of the Sky." Dee had said that it was located in the mountains above Malibu Beach and from the direction in which Chad was flying, Dee's information was correct. Already they had passed over Laurel, Benedict, and Coldwater canyons, three of the principal paths leading from the heavily populated San Fernando Valley over the Santa Monica Mountains and into West Hollywood and Beverly Hills. Below them Katherine could see great swaths of heavily treed parklike areas interrupted here and there by impressive roof lines and further augmented by complementing abstract shapes colored an exquisite turquoise blue. They were flying over the estates of Beverly Hills and Bel-Air and the bits of blue twinkling in the hot sunlight like so many pieces of beautifully colored glass were the swimming pools of the very, very rich. The horizon line was growing rapidly into a wider and wider stripe of shimmering ocean. Malibu could not be far away.

Katherine's eyes tracked the tiny dots sprinkled over the golden sand and the antlike automobiles that filled the beach-bound streets and freeways. As many people as could manage to do so were escaping the inland heat.

Filling the bluffs above the beach and edging the ocean's

sand, high-priced homes stood cheek by jowl. Katherine watched the sea of humanity that pushed against the ocean's edge and felt very small and unimportant.

Suddenly, as if responding directly to her secret cry for solitude, Chad veered the helicopter away from the Pacific, and Katherine saw the encroachment of civilization abruptly stopped. Scenery changed to rolling green spotted with a handful of tiny lakes and, in the blaze of late fall, sun-parched meadows.

Chad swooped them low as they neared the only sign of habitation. It was a rectangle of adobe and warm Mexican tiles snugly nestled amid an ancient grove of California live oaks. The landing pad was situated discreetly to the south and east of the hacienda, and Chad dropped them onto it as lightly as if the helicopter had been a butterfly.

They had arrived and Katherine's heart began pounding irregularly. She had made up her mind not to leave the seat of the helicopter, and as long as she kept her seat belt fastened she felt quite safe. When Chad tired of looking at her sitting there in the cockpit, he would give in and take her back. There could be no other way.

As soon as the huge propeller blade stopped, Chad jumped from his seat without speaking and silently loped around to where Katherine sat, arms folded across her chest. Through the glass his dark eyes reached out and held her motionless. Still without speaking, Chad swung the door open, reached in, and with one easy motion disengaged the seat belt and with the next motion was lifting Katherine into his arms and bringing her from the cockpit to the wall of his broad chest.

Katherine found herself unable to move her eyes from his, and as he brought her closer and closer she knew exactly what must happen, and she was so torn between wanting and not wanting that to resist became impossible.

51

"Welcome to Cielo."

As Chad spoke Katherine's eyes slid down to his lips and watched them as they came to meet her own. The line of his mouth was strong and smooth, but his lips were determined and dominating. They insisted on total control and demanded that she abandon all the defenses she had learned as a part of growing up.

It was a long and telling kiss that began quietly and grew in probing demand and helpless submission until at last Katherine realized that beyond her conscious will her arms had wrapped themselves around Chad's strong neck to pull him closer and still she could not get enough of him. Her lips clung to his and would have gone on doing so had not Chad ended the moment by allowing her long legs to drift from his arms until she found firm ground beneath her and could stand alone.

"Hmm," Chad murmured huskily, "I like it."

Katherine looked up, and the expression in his eyes frightened her back to the reality of the moment. Frantically she began to beat her hands against his chest and try to push herself away from him so that there could be no further danger.

"Let me go! Let me go!" she cried in genuine alarm. "What kind of a man are you to lure me up here, pretending it's all for business, and then do this? Take me back now!"

Katherine spun away from him and attempted to climb back into the helicopter, but Chad grabbed her arm and whirled her about to face him, his fingers pressing mercilessly into her soft flesh.

"Don't tell me you didn't like it," Chad insisted, his eyes suddenly cold and filled with danger.

"I do tell you!" Katherine tossed her mane of hair defiantly.

"Then your words lie," he sneered. "Look at me!" He

shook her until she obeyed. "I'm no schoolboy, Katherine Dunn." Now the mocking sneer was even more obvious. "I know how to read a woman's desires, and you're filled with them."

Katherine started to protest and again Chad shook her into obedience.

"Just be sure of this, any time I want I can force those flailing arms of yours beneath you and show you just how filled with want that luscious body of yours is."

Katherine was quivering all over, knowing that no matter how much she might try to deny it Chad Butler was right. He had proved it to her, and now half of her was afraid that he would take advantage of his knowledge and the other half feared that he would not.

He must have felt her trembling because he dropped his hold on her abruptly and changed his manner completely. Once again he was the efficient businessman.

"Don't worry," he told her. "I'm not going to rape you. It isn't my style." Coolly he turned his back on her and proceeded to secure the helicopter, allowing Katherine the much-needed time to smooth her ruffled appearance and try futilely to restore her inner calm. When he returned to her, it was with his familiar charming smile and the same courteous manner he might use with Eleanor Graham. Katherine scolded herself that instead of feeling relief she felt disappointment.

"Let's not stand out here in the hot sun," Chad said smoothly as though their previous encounter had never occurred. "I want to show you the house."

Very politely, and very firmly, Chad took her arm and directed her up away from the landing area and toward Casa del Cielo.

Katherine had been too absorbed with the man to take notice of his home, but now that she did she saw instantly why it was so named. Casa del Cielo, "House of the Sky," sat on a smooth, natural knoll, its roof line the same level as the surrounding treetops. Above the house and the rolling hills the azure-blue sky filled the viewer's eyes so completely that it was easy to believe that here indeed was a slice of heaven.

Katherine gave a little gasp of pleasure, and Chad looked down at her, clearly pleased with her reaction.

"Do you like it?" he asked.

"Yes." She sighed, so totally entranced with the tranquillity of the scene before her that for a moment she forgot the very earth-bound feelings Chad had aroused within her. "Even in my dreams I've never seen anything like it."

The building was obviously old, very old for the West. Even Katherine's untutored eye recognized it as being authentically from the California mission era. Long, low adobe walls were crowned with red tiles whose uneven shaping proclaimed them to be handcast. The slant of the shed roof allowed for a broad overhang, which, when supported as it was by the massive lintels and rough-hewn posts, formed a charming rim of shaded porch. Vivid crimson bougainvillea and star-white jasmine provided a colorful and fragrant frame, while within, cushioned wood benches and potted greenery beckoned alluringly.

Katherine wanted to stop here and sink into one of the gaily striped cushions but Chad's firm grasp of her arm propelled her insistently forward to the huge carved oak doorway. Opening the door, Chad led her over the wide threshold and into the cool and restful interior.

Inside, the light was dim. It was several seconds before Katherine's eyes made the adjustment, and when she could focus again, it was to the realization that the door had been closed behind them and that no matter how enchanting she might find the hacienda she was helplessly shut inside, alone with its master. Nervously Katherine

54

stepped away from Chad and backed toward a wall, as though its blank surface could protect her from his alarming virility.

"You look like a scared rabbit." He laughed and moved a step closer, his lips twisting in contempt. "Don't worry." He turned his back on her and walked casually into the living room. "I won't sneak up on you. As I said, when I make love to you, you'll be wanting it more than I do. As for now," he continued, gesturing for her to join him, "I did bring you up here for business as well as the pleasure of watching you squirm."

Katherine did not know which aspect of Chad's behavior disturbed her the most: his brazen way of grabbing her and making use of her as he wished or this brand of arrogant scorn. And beyond that she could not understand why this man's obnoxious behavior fascinated her more than it repelled her.

"Well?" he called out impatiently. "Are you going to stand out in the entry all day, or are you going to come in and behave like the sensible, cool-headed businesswoman you would like everyone to think you are?"

Meekly she obeyed. Chad had all the cards in his hand; it would be silly of her to resist.

When Katherine reached the living room, she was surprised to find that he had a whole stack of publications, still photographs, and business memos neatly stacked on the rustic coffee table.

"I brought this up last night," Chad told her and then, seeing her puzzlement, went on to explain that he lived at the ranch most of the time. "I have a place down in town," he added. "That's where I do most of my entertaining."

Katherine sent him a sidewise glance. Entertained women most likely, she thought, and was surprised at the wave of jealousy that overcame her.

During the next two hours Chad went over the materi-

55

als he had gathered and further explained what he was looking for in the forthcoming sales promotion and why he thought Katherine could be of help.

"You know that little encounter we had yesterday made me curious to find out exactly what kind of people we are hiring these days," he said with a sardonic twist to his lips that infuriated Katherine. "Well, even you have to admit that you chose an unusual way to introduce yourself."

"I did nothing of the sort," Katherine snapped testily. "It was a complete accident and you know it."

Chad's sly smile grew wider as he raised his hands in a gesture of innocence. "Whatever you say. But I still found it unusual. So I went up to personnel and found your file."

Katherine flinched. It was dreadful to be caught in a position where you had no privacy.

Chad seemed to realize her irritation and he surveyed her slowly with a raised eyebrow before he continued. "This has nothing to do with your physical attractions. This is strictly business. If you can perform as well as your references say, then you could be a real asset to us. If not, well, that's when we will discuss your other . . . talents."

The way in which he allowed his eyes to rove, lingering on the full curve of her breasts, as he discussed her "talents" was so insultingly familiar that Katherine could not trust herself to answer him. Instead she rose from the couch and turned away from him, denying him the pleasure of seeing her fury. Somehow, Katherine sensed, allowing herself to become angry would only incite him. It was best to remain quiet no matter how much she wanted to tell this impossible egotist exactly what she thought of him.

"You're right," Chad said in a maddeningly calm voice that totally ignored her obvious wrath. "We've been sitting here for too long a time. Let's go outside and get some fresh air. Besides, I want to show you where I want the photographic locations to be." He stood and stretched, his lithe movements reminding Katherine, uncomfortably, of some wild predator who only wore a thin coat of civilized manners, a coat that could be shed without warning to reveal the untamable passions that lay beneath.

Outside, adjacent to the hacienda, was a low building that housed all the farming implements needed to run the ranch. Katherine recognized tractors and a variety of trucks, but there were several other machines whose uses she could not discern. Chad led the way to a dusty pickup and helped her to climb into the cab.

As he opened the door Katherine surveyed the less than pretentious appearance with a skeptical eye. "This certainly isn't up to the usual Butler standards," she commented wryly.

"Get in anyway," he told her and gave her backside a resounding slap.

Katherine yelped and sat down quickly, her eyes stinging more with humiliation than pain. "How dare you!" she shouted.

"I can dare a whole lot, honey," he answered smoothly. His implied meaning was absolutely clear and as he swung into the driver's seat he leaned his head so near to Katherine's that she had to veer desperately away in order to avoid his lips.

"Oh, Katherine Dunn, you are a silly goose," he teased, throwing back his head and laughing heartily at her expense.

Once again Katherine felt defeated but she tried to retain a prim decorum by ignoring Chad and looking out the window at her side. The truck's engine turned over and Chad backed it deftly away from the other vehicles and out into the blazing sunshine. She sneaked a look at

Chad and he caught her, returning it with another teasing wink. Katherine returned her gaze to the window and as the truck lurched and bounced over the rocky trail Katherine pondered the oddities of her relationship with Chad Butler and the fact that whenever he called her by her full name he was being clearly derisive.

The air, which moments before had been so clear, was now clouded with dust, and Katherine coughed and sputtered as it seeped up her nose and tickled her throat, until Chad finally took the hint and closed his window.

"Here, use this," he said, handing her his hankerchief. Grateful for this bit of assistance, Katherine blotted her eyes and blew her nose noisily.

"Guess you can see now why the truck's so dusty. Of course, if I'd known you're so particular, I might have given it a washing." He paused and looked at her, grinning insolently at her discomfort. "No, I don't think I would have bothered. Just get dusty again."

Now that her vision had cleared, Katherine could see exactly what Chad was referring to. Everything about the truck, inside as well as outside, was thickly coated with heavy silt. Everything including Katherine's dress, and as she traced a finger trail over her lap, she thought of her hair and patted it, only to realize that it too had been thoroughly covered with dirt.

Chad read the helpless fury of her expression. "Don't worry, it brushes off," he reasoned as the truck tilted over what felt like a boulder of jagged contour.

Katherine was about to protest the insanity of the entire venture when Chad brought them to a jolting halt. She avoided a confrontation with the dashboard only because Chad's strong right arm held her safely in place.

"Sorry," he exclaimed, "but we didn't want to hit that!" He was pointing to a sizable earthen clump directly in front of them from which a few dozen wasp warriors were already angrily emerging. "Another couple of yards and we would have been in real trouble."

Chad shifted the truck into reverse to move around the nest and drove on a short distance further before stopping again and shutting off the motor.

"Here we are," he announced, and when the dust cleared, Katherine saw before them a landscape quite different from that closer to the hacienda. It was a setting that might easily have doubled for the site of the Ming tombs that Chad had shown them all on slides just the previous day. Suddenly Katherine understood perfectly what he was talking about. This was the photographic setting he wanted to use as a backdrop for the silk gowns and fabulous jewelry Butler's would introduce into the American fashion market.

"A little bit of California that looks a lot like China."

"Very convenient," Katherine agreed.

"That's exactly what I thought when I was over there and saw their terrain and knew it was almost exactly like home. It made the whole idea seem like a natural."

"Natural enough to invest nearly two million dollars?"

"Yes," he snapped. Katherine looked over to him and noted the scowl on his face as he studied the landscape before them.

Chad Butler had more than the two million dollars invested in this idea—and his reputation in the business community. If he were to fail, Butler's Board of Directors might well revolt against him. It was a daring idea, filled with potential risk, but no one knew Butler's marketing formula better than Chad, and no one had the right to challenge his decisions.

Katherine turned her gaze to follow Chad's. The better acquainted she became with him the more she found that she admired him. Grudgingly she had to admit even though Chad Butler was an arrogant handful with women he was a brilliant businessman. Handsome too, she admitted, and not for the first time, as she sneaked a sidewise glance at his strong profile. His hands, she noticed, were gripping the wheel so intently that the knuckles were white. Without wanting to, Katherine found her thoughts wandering to memories of his touch, the feel of his fingers upon her skin. She shook herself to clear her head and concentrated determinedly upon the rock-strewn valley.

The hard dry soil had grown increasingly hot as the sun rose in the sky, and now, as she watched, the earth seemed to be sending back some of that heat in shimmering waves that distorted her vision. Nonetheless Katherine could imagine the silk gowns, the pearls, the lustrous jade, all posed against this tableau, and she knew absolutely that Chad's ideas could not fail. She started to tell him so as he turned to face her, but the penetrating expression on his face made her words unnecessary. The moment seemed to startle them both. Katherine could not be sure of Chad's feelings, but she knew for a certainty that never before in her lifetime had she experienced such a feeling of total understanding.

"Come on, you crazy redhead," Chad said as if to relieve the tension this new awareness had caused them both. "I forgot that a paleface like you isn't used to being out of doors."

Katherine did not know what she had expected Chad to say, but certainly this was the very last thing. Paleface? Not used to the out-of-doors? How he had misread her! She could not restrain her laughter.

"I don't know what I said that was so funny," he admitted as he turned the key in the truck's ignition, "but it doesn't matter, because, you know, you're gorgeous when you laugh."

"Why, thank you, kind sir. That's a very nice thing to say."

"Just don't let it go to your head," he admonished, and Katherine had to laugh again.

Their mood of easy camaraderie continued as the truck retraced the ragged path and Katherine found herself regaling Chad with tales of her lumber-town youth. She picked stories from the better days, of course. The time before her father had gone, when he had taught her how to fish sitting on his knee; and the time she had chased a cougar from the hen house with one of her dad's slippers; even those treasured memories of sailboats drifting on a mountain lake. By the time they had reached the Casa all of Katherine's reserve had been wiped away and she was laughing and chatting as easily as when she had been a schoolgirl.

Chad pulled the truck back into the big garage and cut the motor. "I never would have guessed you weren't a city girl," he told her and reached a hand out to her chin. "Maybe that's what I see in those amazing green eyes of yours that's so damned seductive—a genuine, earthy, down-home gal."

Katherine stiffened. Familiarity was dangerous. All of her defenses fell back into place.

Chad watched the layers of coolness drop between them without changing his expression. "Let's go get ourselves a drink," he suggested, breaking the silence.

"Fine, only let me have a brush first so I can sweep off all this grime."

Chad answered her request and watched without any show of sympathy as Katherine attempted to clear the stubbornly clinging dirt from her clothes. "I thought you said this stuff would brush right off."

He shrugged carelessly. "A woman with your background ought to know that ranch life isn't always tidy."

Katherine glared at him in exasperation. "I've been working at forgetting that for five years."

61

"Oh, come on now. I saw your expression out there when you were looking over the place. You're not the uptight, high-rise type. You've got the wide open spaces in your blood."

"There're some things I like about it," she admitted begrudgingly as she caught sight of the oak trees and rolling hills through the open garage door. "But I like my creature comforts better. All I want right now is that cool drink you promised and a fast trip back to where I can clean up and change."

Chad had been standing resting his weight against a post, his well-muscled arms folded across his broad chest. His eyes were twinkling at her mischievously. She was getting to know his expressions, and this one told her that he had a plan afoot and she had better move carefully.

This time, as they returned to the house, Katherine determined to keep Chad's attention on being a good host. That ought to keep him busy until they were ready to leave.

When they had been working in the living room, she had been too nervous and too involved in Chad's ideas to give the interior more than a cursory look. Now, as Chad led her back to the same couch and left her alone while he went for the drinks, she studied her surroundings carefully. Everything, every detail, reflected the presence of a strong and commanding man who liked a straightforward approach to life and held a deep aversion to subterfuge and artifice.

The warm, earthen colors and rustic handmade furniture gave the home a comfortable look that in no way detracted from the fine Mexican antiques and artifacts that studded the rooms like priceless jewels. The huge living room seemed to be designed around a lighted glass column that stood in the center and acted as a divider between two conversational groupings of chairs and couches. Inside the lighted column was a series of rectangular glass shelves, and on each shelf fascinating treasures of pre-Columbian art were displayed.

Katherine's eyes roved beyond the living room, noticing that a wall separated this area from the hacienda's main hall at one end, while on the opposite side a wall of glass revealed a delightful patio that filled the center of the area around which the hacienda had been built. Katherine rose and went over to the glass to look out upon the picture-postcard scene. There were small citrus trees to provide islets of aromatic shade and colorful tubs of geranium, gardenia, lobelia, and hibiscus. At the very heart was a classically proportioned pool whose waters reflected the clear blue of the sky.

"Looks tempting, doesn't it?" Chad said, handing her a tall frosted glass of minted tea.

Once again Katherine became aware of the dramatic effect Chad's physical nearness had upon her. As far as she was concerned, there were entirely too many temptations lurking dangerously about, and she moved over to the lighted column for protection.

"You have quite a collection here."

"Ummm. Oh, yes." Chad's attentions had seemed far too involved with Katherine's figure, and she mentioned the group of figures in hopes of breaking the pattern of his thoughts.

"Where do they all come from?" she asked encouragingly.

Chad stepped over to join her, defeating her efforts to avoid being so near to him.

"They all come from ancient Mexico," he said, standing directly behind her so that his warm breath crept through her hair and caused every nerve ending to tingle. "Those fat little dogs are from Colima. That sleek-looking female

63

figure is Nayarit and the mask over there, the one tatooed in turquoise, is Olmec."

Katherine could feel Chad's hand brush against her waist, and realizing what could take place, she slipped past him and moved into a more open area.

"Don't you think it's time we left?" she asked, trying to sound calm.

"There's no hurry." Chad's lips twisted sardonically. "Come on. Let me at least show you the rest of the place."

There was no way she could politely refuse his offer and so she resigned herself to following him down the hall. Before she knew it the spell of the Casa had caught hold of her.

"How old is Cielo?" she asked.

"The foundations and original walls date back to the seventeen thirties," he told her. "Can you imagine all of the life this place has seen?"

Katherine nodded. Visions of Spanish senoritas with their flashing black eyes and delectable golden skin, rattling their castanets and flouncing silken petticoats, swirled before her eyes. Following them came the clomping boots and melodic tinkle of silvery spurs as the lean, dark vaqueros entered. She looked at Chad and for a moment he was like one of those earlier men and she wanted him to sweep her up into his embrace as she knew those earlier women had been swept. She blushed at the boldness of her thoughts and made an effort to change the subject.

"Was it in very bad condition when you bought it?"

"Terrible!" He laughed, shaking his head at the memory. "It was a complete ruin, only a few falling-down sections of the outer wall remained. Thank heaven the foundations were still pretty much intact. From them I was able to reconstruct what the original hacienda had been. I made a few changes like the glass wall and swimming pool, also I added some of your kind of creature comforts—electricity, indoor plumbing, air conditioning."

"You?" Katherine's eyes grew round with surprise. "Are you saying that you built all of this?"

Chad offered her a callused hand to inspect. "Sure did." He grinned and then his smile faded. "When I got home from Vietnam, I needed something constructive to do with my hands—something to build after all of that destruction. You might say that this was my own kind of therapy. It worked too. I love this place almost as much as I love women."

He was teasing her again. She would soon call a permanent end to this charade and insist on returning to Butler's. Chad could not have any further excuses for keeping her here.

He was guiding her past the splendid dining area, pointing out the furniture that had come from Europe to be placed in the ill-fated court of Maximilian and Carlota. They came to the first corner of the rectangular design and Katherine saw that the kitchen was immediately on the other side. She tried unsuccessfully to repress a sigh. The room was designed and equipped to fulfill the dreams of every cook.

"Like to cook, hum?" Chad observed.

"Didn't I boast?" she bantered. "I placed in a Four-H competition. But"—she shrugged—"I haven't had much of a chance to practice lately."

"Maybe we can do something about that," he answered, refilling her glass with tea. "In the meantime come with me."

". . .'said the spider to the fly,' " Katherine whispered to herself, following him anyway and finding herself in a pleasant room filled with potted plants and rattan furniture.

"This is where I like to sit and put my feet up," Chad told her, leading her around the second corner, "because it's so convenient to my personal quarters."

That was all of the warning Katherine had before she found herself being ushered into Chad Butler's bedroom suite. Three steps inside the door and she stopped, frozen with apprehension.

"What's wrong?" Chad asked, his voice mocking her. "Never been in a man's bedroom before?"

Katherine stepped back out. She did not care what he said or even what he thought of her. She had seen enough: his huge fur-covered bed, the wall of mirrors behind it, and Chad himself standing there exuding his undeniable sensuality. She could not allow herself to be caught in that room alone with him.

"It's time you took me back to the store," she told him calmly, barely managing to keep her raging pulse from entering into her voice.

Chad followed her into the hall and eyed her keenly. "You never have been in a man's room, have you?"

Katherine saw no point in answering his insolent question. Instead she started back toward the study.

"Hey, wait," he called after her, "I'll take you back, just as you asked."

"You will?" She turned to face him, surprised at how easily he had agreed.

"Certainly." He took the iced tea from her and put both of their glasses on a nearby table. Then, sweeping both of her hands into an implacable grip, he pulled her closer. "I'll take you right back, just as soon as we have a little swim."

"Swim?" she cried incredulously. "I can't swim. I don't have a bathing suit."

Chad tilted his head and looked almost coy. "You don't need a swimsuit at Cielo. Skinny-dipping is the rule here."

Katherine gasped, genuinely shocked.

"Well," he said, pouting his lip in mock-disappointment. "I suppose rules are made for exceptions. Come back over here, I'm sure I have something that'll fit you quite nicely."

Since he still held a firm grip on her hands, Katherine had no choice but to follow, and when he let go of her to open a hallway cupboard, she saw at a glance that for once Chad had not been teasing her. There must have been more than a dozen suits of various colors and sizes. They all had one thing in common: their scantiness.

"Here you go." He offered her an emerald maillot. "This should be perfect."

Katherine tried to protest but Chad was deliberately refusing to listen. Instead he pushed her gently but firmly into his bedroom. "Now you just be a good little girl and go in here and change. I'll meet you in the swimming pool."

"Persistent, aren't you?" Katherine snapped, knowing that she had lost another round.

"You might say so." Chad's smile was definitely rakish. "I'm used to getting exactly what I want."

CHAPTER FOUR

Katherine closed the door firmly and checked the latch. She could not be sure just how trustworthy Chad was when it came to someone else's privacy. She slipped out of the yellow dress and wrinkled her nose disgustedly at the garment's pathetic state. The one good thing about going for a swim was that all of the dirt and stickiness would be gone. Katherine walked through Chad's large dressing room and into his bath. A quick shower would be just the ticket. After rinsing herself off, she felt a thousand times better. She grabbed an extra towel and, after drying herself, took it with her; it would be useful out by the pool.

Back in Chad's bedroom the wall of mirrors was unavoidable. Katherine saw herself blush to the roots of her red hair. How many other women, she wondered, had viewed themselves like this?

She had analyzed the good and bad of her body before but somehow the absolute maleness of this room and the vastness of the mirrors made her nakedness seem so much more obvious.

Her skin, she knew, was one of her best assets. Though translucently pale and refusing ever to tan, it held a creamy color that set off the rich vibrance of her copper hair and sea-green eyes very nicely indeed. Katherine allowed her hands to drift down over her sides and hips. Her figure was something to be grateful for too. There had been enough compliments from men over the years to establish that as a fact in her mind, and there was no denying that it was quite gratifying to know that men found her desirable. Her long legs were well proportioned, slim, and shapely; and she excused her exceptionally broad shoulders as being proper for a woman of her height. The curves, however, were not as generous as she would have liked. Katherine frowned at her small breasts. Well, at least they were high and firm. All considered, she decided as she patted her flat stomach, it was not bad. The nose and mouth might not pass the experts' judgment, but the rest of her was passable.

Chad's choice, the green maillot suit, fit her like a second skin except that it left a great deal of her own white flesh exposed, especially in the back where the maillot barely managed to cover her buttocks. Tying the thin ribbon of a strap securely around her neck, she wondered exactly for whom Chad had purchased the cupboard full of swimwear and if, as he had stated, skinny-dipping really was a frequent pastime at Cielo.

She gave herself a final review in the mirror. Would Chad find her as attractive as all of the other women he entertained? She shook herself. Why should she care? She was only doing this to be a good sport. After all, the only relationship she wanted to have with Chad Butler was purely and strictly business. But as she turned away from the mirrors Katherine had the very distinct feeling that she was going to have to remind herself of that fact again and again in the future.

Deliberately she ran her hand over the springy hairs of the wolf skins that covered his bed. How appropriate, she thought as the stiff outer hairs tantalized her fingertips. Moving them back and revealing the downy undercoat, she recognized the heavy fragrance of musk that suddenly wafted up to invade her nostrils. Katherine shivered involuntarily. The feel of him was everywhere: in the air she breathed; the dark wood bookshelves filled with papers and books; the antique armoire that, she had already discovered, housed his hunting clothes; and then there was this enormous bed with its sensual animal covering.

Watch out, Katherine admonished herself. *Get yourself out of here before the very atmosphere seduces you.* But something on one of the bedside tables caught her attention: a photo of a family group that was simply framed with a walnut border. Posed at the rear was a tall, aristocratic man standing proudly behind his beautiful wife, and before them sat two smiling boys, as alike as two peas. Which one was Chad? Katherine wondered. And which one was the twin who had died with this stately woman who had been their mother?

When she stepped out into the strong sunlight, Chad was nowhere in sight. Remembering that he had told her to meet him at the pool, she crossed over to its brightly tiled edge. Again she looked for Chad. Should she wait or should she go ahead? The hot, still air gave her the answer. She poised for a moment at the edge and dove in, cutting the water like a long slender blade.

The pool, she was glad to note, was especially designed for swimming laps. And now, as she emerged from her dive, Katherine went into a smooth glide across the surface, counting her strokes out of old habit. As a girl she had won a number of local meets, and the hours spent in practice and actual competition were the best memories she had of the years following her father's desertion. The time at the lake had meant less time spent listening to her mother's bitter monologues. And her mother, eager and delighted to see Katherine succeed, had never questioned her daughter's motives but instead had proudly attributed Katherine's poise and figure to the endless hours of practice.

The coolness of the water served as a tonic for her lagging energy and when, at last, she paused, it was not because she was tired but rather because she wanted to savor her pleasure.

A green and yellow float lay at the pool's edge. Katherine pulled it to her, climbed aboard, and allowed herself to drift while lazily dangling her fingers in the water. She would have relaxed entirely had not disturbing thoughts of her absent host continued to cause her confusion. Where was he? she wondered. What could be taking him so long? At length the high noon sun and gently swaying float had their way and Katherine was lulled into drowsiness. Even the provocative image of Chad's dark face could no longer hold her need for sleep at bay, and stretching like a well-fed cat, Katherine allowed herself to drift into a peaceful nap.

Suddenly a cold spray of water fell across her back, accompanied by a newly familiar voice, and for an instant Katherine thought that indeed her dreams were haunted.

"Wake up!" the low, laughing voice called as another arc of water fell. "Hey, Sleeping Beauty, wake up!"

Katherine lifted her head and saw Chad standing tall as a mythical giant and brown as the bark on one of the oaks. Was this another image to recklessly invade her sleep?

Almost soundlessly Chad sprang into the pool, and in a moment his dark head, shining with wetness, rose up beside her.

"What are you doing, lounging about?" he asked, faking a severity that the glitter in his eyes and playful twist of his wide mouth belied. "I said we were going to swim, and swim it is!" A well-muscled arm reached out and tilted Katherine off the float.

Katherine nearly choked as she went under. Chad had caught her off guard, but beneath the water she was as confident and able as a seal. Easily she slipped from his outstretched hands and swam away, emerging through the surface with a laugh.

Chad was right behind her. "You're a good swimmer," he exclaimed with obvious surprise as he stood up next to her.

"I know," she bantered, trying desperately to overcome the unnerving effect that being so close to him was having upon her usually disciplined calm. Shyly she looked up into his face, and the smoldering sensuality she saw there startled her into action.

"You said you wanted to swim," she cried, splashing water at him while she gained a little distance. "So let's get to it."

Swiftly she pushed off from the end of the pool, and praying that she had not forgotten her old technique, she propelled herself forward and away from any chance that Chad might reach out to stop her. But that, it seemed, was not his intent. Instead he was swimming in the lane beside her, keeping her pace with casual ease. The harder she tried to move ahead of him the more frustrated she became. This time Katherine did not even try to count the laps. She swam on and on until her arms and legs were like tallow and her lungs screamed for rest. She pulled herself out of the pool and sat on the rim, sucking in great gasps of air and watching Chad swim lazily on and on.

Katherine was a strong swimmer and she knew it, yet once again Chad had shown her that she was no match for him. He could outdistance her here just as easily as he could outmaneuver her in other situations. Nonetheless, she realized with some surprise, rather than resenting his supremacy, she liked it.

Water trickled down her nose. She smoothed back her hair and allowed the wetness to cascade down her back, but not for a moment could she pull her eyes from the swimmer.

What a splendid body he had! Not that she was surprised. The way in which he wore his clothes had promised that. Yet, she had to admit, seeing him like this with his broad-shouldered, heavily muscled physique was again stirring those restless feelings within her—those strange and new feelings that had been preoccupying her thoughts ever since their first dramatic encounter in Butler's foyer.

As though he sensed her secret turmoil, Chad swam to where she waited, lifting his head and shoulders out of the water directly between her feet. The water on his skin made it glisten like bronze satin, and Katherine flushed at her impulse to reach out and touch him. In quick defense she darted her eyes to his face, but that was no defense at all. His dark eyes were flaming with their need for her.

"I tried to stay away," he murmured huskily and slipped his hands around her ankles.

At the very touch of his fingers she began to tremble visibly. Chad wasted no more words. Firmly but gently he brought her yielding body down into the water beside him. His powerful hands had followed the contours of her body, moving up her legs and thighs, over her hips, past her waist, teasing the full curve of her breasts, and gripping her shoulders until he could guide her into the embrace she had so feared and now, in a matter of seconds, found that she wanted more than anything in the world.

Blindly Katherine turned her face, her lips seeking his as they came down to possess her. There was nothing tentative this time in the way Chad pulled her closer and closer until the softness of her body was crushed against his and she could feel the rigid tension of his muscles beneath her fingertips. His lips, too, were bruising, and as his hold upon her tightened, Katherine became increasingly aware of his consuming need for her and a fiery passion burst within her, spurring her on to a response she had never realized she was capable of giving.

Chad groaned and as Katherine clung to him, digging her fingers into the flesh of his shoulders, his mouth moved away from hers and she felt a hot thrill run the entire length of her body as his lips glided over her cheek, down her neck, across her shoulder.

He was not going to stop. His mouth, hot with desire, was tracing a path ever downward and for one gloriously wild moment Katherine wanted him to go on. Then, entirely against her will, a voice came crowding into her mind, obliterating everything, even Chad's exquisite nearness. It was Eleanor's voice saying over and over: ". . . just a toy to amuse him . . . just a toy . . . nothing special."

Somehow she found the strength to pull away. Frantically she made her way to the steps, but Chad was right behind her.

"Katherine, Katherine," he was calling in a husky half whisper. "I need you. Don't leave me."

He grabbed for her and pulled her back to him. This time his hands were rough. His hold upon her was all strength and there was no gentle tenderness, only urgent, insistent demand.

"Let me go! Let me go! I don't want any of this!" Katherine screamed. With unexpected suddenness Chad released her and she scurried hurriedly to climb out of the pool. Moving quickly to where she had left her towel, she saw the red marks on her arms and shoulders. They were from Chad's hands and she wondered if her face was bruised too.

A vigorous toweling helped to mask her violent trembling. Both her mind and body were tormented by the wild waves of emotions Chad had released in her. Part of her wanted to return to his embrace, to go on forever enjoying the delights of his kisses. But the sensible half of her knew that must never be. Eleanor was right. Chad was a practiced lover and she had far too much pride ever to allow herself to become any man's plaything—even a man as desirable as Chad Butler.

"You teasing, conniving little temptress! Of all the despicable tricks women like you are capable of, this is one of the worst!"

Chad had followed her out of the pool and grabbed her arm in a grip of steel. Ruthlessly he twisted her to face him. Katherine's eyes grew wide with fright as she saw the rigid set of his jaw and the sneering line of anger on his mouth, which only moments earlier had been caressing her body into a flight of ectasy. She knew his scathing attack was by no means over.

"Look at you, you redheaded she-devil! Even now playing the role. Standing there all innocent with those big green eyes so wide, so filled with maidenly virtue, while that body of yours won't quit tempting!"

His eyes were two hot coals of burning fury as they swept ferociously over her, lingering hungrily upon the most intimate areas of her body.

"It's your fault!" she lashed back in a desperate defense. "You're the one who gave me this suit to wear. You're the one who brought me here and insisted upon this insane sw—" Tears filled her eyes. "Let me go!" she pleaded. "You're hurting me."

"Hurting you? Good! At least you're capable of one

human feeling," Chad snarled, grasping her free hand with vicious force.

The salty taste of tears seeped between Katherine's lips, stinging at the bruises that Chad's passion had wrought and igniting her own Irish fury.

"You brute!" she seethed, her pearly teeth flashing like small daggers. "You wretched, miserable excuse for a man. Take your hands off me this instant!"

"My, my." He leered at her, bringing his face dangerously close. "You're quite the consummate actress, aren't you? First it was the passion play and now it's outraged maidenhood, complete with stock phrases and crocodile tears."

"You are a beast!" Katherine cried up at him as she squirmed uselessly in a futile fight to free herself.

"Perhaps," he answered with deceptive mildness. "A moment ago you called me a 'wretched, miserable excuse for a man.' Why don't I show you exactly the kind of man I am?" His eyes made his meaning absolutely clear as he brought both of Katherine's wrists together in one of his hands, thus freeing the other to rove roughly down her bare back and finger threateningly the edge of her suit where it began its scant coverage. "Then," he continued, "you can decide for yourself."

"No! No! Please, no!" Katherine sobbed in fright.

Chad responded by forcing her body to mold to his, pulling her tight, lifting her arching back inward and up so that their lips were almost touching. Then, with the same degree of cruel fierceness, he flung her from him, and Katherine fell to the ground, looking up at him like a helpless penitent pleading for mercy.

"You're like a bright bit of fruit," he told her, his voice filled with disgust. "Sweet at first taste but poisonous at the core." He stooped over the towel Katherine had dropped when he first grabbed her, picked it up, and threw it at her derisively.

"Get dressed," he ordered, "and I'll get you out of here."

Moving as quickly as her rubbery legs would allow, Katherine rushed for the house and the safety of Chad's room. Once inside she closed the heavy door and leaned against it, wishing with all of her heart that the words and events of the last hour could be erased forever from her mind.

What was she going to do? Never had she been treated so by a man, and yet . . .

Katherine trembled all over recalling the feel of Chad's lips, warm and firm, upon her own. Against her will her fingers traced the burning path those lips had taken over her cheek, down her neck, across her shoulder. What would have happened if Eleanor's message had not intervened? She dared not think of that too carefully. Yet the possibilities persisted in teasing her, and she blushed at her own imagination. Even the bruising memory of Chad's fierce and raging abuse refused to diminish the tingling sensual awareness his passion had aroused. She threw her head back and breathed deeply. She was still too badly shaken to attempt dressing.

Slowly Katherine gathered the strength to tread the necessary steps to Chad's bed, where her clothing lay waiting. She stripped off the emerald suit and began to wrap it in the towel, then she paused, recalling the provocative vibrancy the suit had evoked as it had shimmered in Chad's hand. Now it was sodden and lifeless, turned almost black by its wetness, and all of the delectable iridescent gleam was gone.

Determinedly Katherine finished wrapping it and set the damp bundle firmly aside just as she knew she must firmly set aside all of the intimacy that had occurred between herself and Chad Butler. It was her only hope of regaining the businesslike relationship she sought to have with him.

Turning back to the bed, Katherine reached out for her clothing. Suddenly, without a sound of warning, the door to the room swung open and Chad Butler stood there, leaning his tall angular body with studied casualness against the doorjamb.

Katherine turned white with shock. She had seen that he could be cruel when angered, but this vile act was more than she would ever have attributed to him. Miraculously she preserved enough calm to guard her obvious vulnerability and with one quick motion swept her garments up protectively about herself.

"How dare you!" she whispered through clenched teeth.

"I told you, I dare plenty." There was more than a hint of menace in his voice, but Katherine did not quaver. "Besides," Chad went on, "I wanted to see if you were a real flesh and blood woman or just acting that part too."

Moments passed as they stared at each other without speaking. Then Chad sent his eyes moving at a deliberate crawl up and down the length of Katherine's body, finally returning his attention to her face and giving her an insolent grin.

"You've seen. Now get out!" Her words were spoken smoothly and without a trace of fear.

"Stop faking it, Katherine Dunn. You want me as much as I want you."

Katherine did not answer. Instead she gave him a look of hostile disdain that was as withering as a freezing wind.

Chad clenched and unclenched his fists. "All right, I'll go, but get this into that scheming brain of yours: Once I'm gone, I'm not coming back and the only future contact between us will be in the line of business—strictly business."

CHAPTER FIVE

It came as no surprise to Katherine that Eleanor Graham now thought the worst of her.

"There's no fool like an overly ambitious young woman who has set her sights too high," Eleanor had hooted at her the morning after her return from Cielo.

"Chad tells me the two of you took care of a lot of business. Hah!" she scoffed. "I know your kind of business, and I'd fire you in a minute"—she snapped her fingers for emphasis—"but Chad says you're going to be 'useful' to him." Another harsh laugh. "Just remember it doesn't take Chad long to become bored."

Eleanor stopped talking and glared at Katherine through narrowed eyes. "As long as you're around," she continued, "I plan to keep you busy. Here's a list of things that need doing."

Every task on Eleanor's list proved to be unpleasant, but by Friday, when Dee caught up to Katherine during their coffee break, Katherine was working on the last and most tedious assignment: cleaning a tall stack of ink-stained overlays.

"If it's any comfort to you, Katherine, I think the old girl's going around the bend," Dee observed as she sipped the dregs from her plastic cup. She had brought up the coffee, knowing that Eleanor had arranged Katherine's schedule so that there were no breaks.

Katherine looked up from her labors and brushed back a fallen strand of hair, smudging ink on her forehead in the process.

"You know, Dee, I wouldn't mind so much if I thought these were going to be used again." She took a swallow of cold coffee and grimaced. "But that's impossible. At least half are torn beyond repair and the rest are hopelessly old and cracking."

Dee looked down at her hands and heaved a guilty sigh. "I'm sorry for getting you into this, Katherine. Believe me, I had no idea Eleanor would be like this! A little difficult, perhaps, but not impossible. Honestly, I don't see how you can make a go of it now."

"Well, I'm not going to quit if that's what you're suggesting." Katherine's voice was firmly determined as she bent back over her task. "And Eleanor is not going to fire me, either. Not so long as Chad Butler wants me working on his promotion."

"But that's just it. Oh, dear, Katherine, I hate to be the one to say this." Dee was wincing at her own words. "You haven't heard a word from him since Wednesday. Maybe he's changed his mind."

You're wrong, Katherine thought to herself and rubbed harder on the ink-stained plastic. She had not told Dee about her encounter with Chad at Cielo. She could not bring herself to tell anyone about the events of that day. Yet it had all turned out just the way she wanted it, hadn't it? Hadn't Chad said himself that their relationship would be "strictly business"? She refused to consider why her heart felt so empty. As for Eleanor, she and Chad were an

80

impossible combination and he knew it. Chad needed her and she was going to be there when he called.

"Give me a little credit for deviousness, Dee," she told her friend. "My plan is to make myself indispensable, and our Mr. Butler has given me just the chance to do it." She stood and stretched.

"He liked my ideas when we discussed them at Cielo. So I have spent the past two nights putting them down on paper—even worked up some mock newspaper ads."

Dee raised her eyebrows appreciatively.

Katherine nodded. She was rather proud of her cleverness.

"Yes, I put the whole package together, wrapped it all up, tied it with—well, not ribbon—string, and placed it on his desk before he arrived this morning."

Dee whistled. "Well? Don't keep me in suspense! What has he said?"

"Nothing!" Katherine lamented. "Not a word."

"Maybe he hasn't seen it yet." Dee was hopeful.

"That's what I keep telling myself." Katherine put the newly cleaned overlay aside and tackled the next one. "All I can do is wait."

She waited until late in the day, every hour becoming a greater agony. What had happened? Didn't he like her work? Had he thrown it aside; or had Eleanor, by some horrid twist of fate, found the package and destroyed it?

At four o'clock the door swung open and Chad Butler strolled into the room. Katherine's heart fluttered at the very sight of him, but he did not even look in her direction. The art director greeted him with obvious pleasure. It was always a great day when the boss dropped by.

Chad stopped and spoke with every person in the department, but still he took no notice of Katherine. After several minutes he turned and, with the art director still at this elbow, started back toward the door. Katherine panicked. He was going to leave without saying a word. She had to do something.

She gave a cough. It was easy to do, considering the noxious fumes of the solvent she was using. Once she started, however, she found she could not stop. The coughs came from deeper and deeper, wrenching her lungs and seriously threatening the calm of her stomach. Still she could not stop. Her eyes filled with tears, and breathing became difficult.

"Open the window and let me get her out of here!" a deep voice commanded imperiously.

Katherine felt herself being lifted, shifted over a shoulder, and carried out ignominiously, like a sack of potatoes.

Chad carted her to a window in the outer hall and, after setting her upon her wobbling legs, supported her in his arms so that her face was close to the flow of fresh air.

"I seem to always be carrying you somewhere, don't I?" he said in an amused voice. "What are you doing up here in the first place? I've had a call out for you all day and no one has known where you were."

Katherine tried to speak but started coughing again.

Chad's arms about her tightened. "Don't talk," he commanded. "Listen for a change." His voice leveled off to a more normal tone. "I like your presentation. Some of your ideas are terrific. Of course they'll need a bit of polish, but on the whole I'm really impressed. And so is Joe. We went over it this morning and I've been trying to find you ever since."

Katherine smiled wanly. This was music to her ears.

"We think Dad should see it," Chad went on, "and we want you to be the one to show it to him. Dad, in case you don't know, lives up in Carmel, and—well—the question is, would you be willing to give up this weekend and fly to Monterey with us tomorrow?"

Katherine could think of only one answer to that question. Saturday morning found her, once again, waiting at the Butler's seventh-floor heliport. Only this time Joe Parkman was there too and they were waiting for a pickup that would deliver them to the international airport.

When they reached the elegant black and gold Falcon jet, Chad welcomed them aboard. "Get yourselves seated," he said. "We're about ready to take off."

As if on cue the engines started their roar and Joe hurried Katherine into the cabin. Buckling herself into her seat, Katherine took a deep breath. Leather! The seats were covered in real leather and they were much more like Eames chairs than airplane passenger seats.

Joe was seated facing her. Between them was a table thoughtfully supplied with sand-filled drink coasters, weighted playing cards, writing paper, and pencils.

"Impressive, isn't it?" Joe asked, smiling his warm, slow smile.

Katherine nodded. "Since I've been working for the Butlers I've seen things I never even knew existed."

"Watch out. It's catching. Five minutes ago you didn't know any of this was here. Five minutes more and you'll be miserable when it's gone."

Chad came in bringing a tray of coffee and sweet rolls. He sat next to Katherine and his eyes moved suspiciously from one to the other.

"You two really get along well, don't you?" he asked.

Joe leaned back in his seat. "Are you jealous?"

"Of course not!" Chad began to bluster, as the sleek little plane gave a slight shudder and taxied down the runway.

Katherine looked out of the window and saw the ground falling away. She found the dimensional transformation both exciting and eerie as all the earthbound symbols she was accustomed to—people, cars, buildings, trees—receded into a topographical design. By the time the plane had finished its ascent and leveled off, they were high above the Pacific and the sails of a regatta appeared as so many white caps on the blue sea.

"Beautiful, isn't it?"

Katherine turned and was startled to find Chad's face so close to her own. His nearness threatened to awaken too many slumbering sentiments, but he seemed unaware of her discomfort.

"The world from here is so at peace, so serene. I'm sure any stranger to our atmosphere would have to think they had found paradise."

Katherine agreed and then noticed they had turned inland and were following the coastline.

"What's that down there?" she asked, pointing to a small cluster of buildings sitting amidst the green rolling countryside.

"San Simeon," Chad answered.

Joe read the question on her face. "San Simeon translates into Hearst Castle, the place that old newspaper tycoon built to house his art collection—and his megalomania."

"Oh, yes!" Katherine exclaimed, her eyes wistful. "I've always wanted to see that. But then"—she shrugged—"there are so many places I've always wanted to see."

"I hope that includes Pebble Beach," Chad said.

"If she's not interested in Pebble Beach, then she's not interested in millionaires," Joe drawled, puffing comfortably on his pipe.

"Pebble Beach? Isn't that where all those famous golf courses are located?" Katherine avoided a direct answer. Why had both of her companions developed ugly ideas about her? Was she cold and calculating or was she a gold digger? Or was she both? There was no point in arguing, because the more she protested, the more determined they would be that they were right. Keeping her thoughts to herself, she spent the remainder of the trip gazing out of the window.

When they landed in Monterey, a satin-black Rolls-Royce, complete with liveried driver, was waiting. The drive from the Peninsula Airport down through the Del Monte Forest to Pebble Beach took roughly twenty minutes. It could have taken forever as far as Katherine was concerned. She was in heaven, seated snugly at the rear of the world's most luxurious car. She was a princess touring her fabulous kingdom. And fabulous it was on this crystal-clear October day with the air crisp and free of the prevalent fog that so often cloaked the woods with mystery. Every glorious detail was there to see: Graceful pine trees intermingled with cedars and firs; and, toward the water's edge, drinking in the salt spray, stood the famous cypress with their gnarled and twisted trunks. Scattered throughout the forest were some of the world's most beautiful homes, and Katherine noticed that each property was named. There was "Old Adobe," "Pinnacle Point," and "Deep Wells."

At last they reached a tall wrought-iron entry that bore the name "Highgates" in gilted letters. The great car glided down the drive through hedges of rhododendron and camellia; past the tennis courts, cabana, and swimming pool; around a bend from where, for the first time, Highgates could be seen.

The sight was enough to take Katherine's breath away. After visiting the rustic splendor of Cielo she had expected something equally Californian here within a few miles of Monterey, the old Spanish capital. Hence her surprise was complete when a mansion out of Henry Tudor's England appeared.

The entire facade was brick, set in the old herringbone design. There was a magnificent arched entry, leaded-glass windows, a slate roof, and seven chimneys. A great oval

85

of grass, taking up at least an acre, preceded the house and was bordered on all sides by the drive. In the middle was a large pond, where wild birds could rest in the course of their hemispheric flights. At one end of the pond, seated on a rock, the bronze figure of a boy gazed eternally into the water.

Katherine leaned toward the front where Chad was seated next to the driver. "Who is that meant to be?" she asked, pointing to the figure.

"Peter Pan," Chad answered, looking over his shoulder. "My mother put it there years ago. She used to say, when my brother and I were young, that we were like the Lost Boys. We didn't want to grow up." He paused and looked out at the little boy receding into the distance. "She was right. We never wanted to leave here—especially Rob."

There was such pain in his voice that Katherine's heart hurt for him. She was not the only one who had lost love.

Joe seemed to sense the melancholy and turned the conversation to golf. By the time the car had pulled under the arches, he and Chad had made plans for a match on the following morning.

Chad left Joe to help Katherine while he mounted the steps to greet his father.

Adam Butler was several inches shorter than his son, and that was not the only difference between them. In photos Katherine had seen he appeared more sensitive and patrician than his rugged son. In person, however, the contrast was quite startling. Where Chad's image was that of a dark giant filled with power and sensuality, Adam's was almost the reverse. His hair and skin were nearly white; and while he was more than six feet tall, he was slender to the point of fragility. In looks he was handsome, but again, quite differently from his son. Adam's features were fine and narrow and when he smiled there was an edge of restraint present. Only the eyes, dark and deep, were like Chad's.

Adam greeted Joe in a manner that showed they had known each other for a long time.

When Chad introduced Katherine, Adam's welcome was old-fashioned and charming in its courtliness. "I am so pleased to see that Eleanor has discovered such a lovely replacement for Mrs. Cummings."

His eyes were filled with kindness as he took Katherine's hands into his own. "Chad tells me that you have brought something very interesting to show me, and I am anxious to see it—but please, no work until after lunch."

Graciously he led Katherine over to where a soberly dressed woman stood waiting in the shadows. "Miss Dunn —Katherine, if I might—this is my housekeeper, Mrs. Chambers. She will show you to your room."

Katherine followed the housekeeper up the broad stairs to the second floor, and she could barely conceal her delight when she was shown to her room. It was heavenly. The kind that any woman, of any age, would adore; its location, overlooking the drive and pond, made it even more enchanting. The walls were papered in yellow with tiny blue cornflowers. The canopied bed and window seat were covered in matching fabric and, together with the filmy crisscross curtains, created the aura of a sunlit garden. Katherine would have enjoyed staying there all day. It was such a contrast to her real home. The others were waiting, however, so she satisfied herself with a quick freshening and went downstairs to join them.

As Adam had promised, their meeting followed lunch and went on for several hours.

Katherine was learning to be comfortable with her "strictly business" relationship with Chad. She certainly was not going to admit to herself that she missed his more special attentions.

Just as Chad and Joe had been enthusiastic about Katherine's ideas, so too was Adam Butler. He was especially pleased with the name she had chosen for the promotion: The China Line.

"It's like By-Line or Main Line," he said. "This is our signature line and by stating it this way we can remove just the one word, China, and replace it for each new promotion."

"That's what I think," Joe agreed. "We can have a Red Line, a Blue Line, even a Timbuktu Line if we want, and as long as the word 'Line' remains constant, our public will pick up on the continuity."

Katherine saw that Chad was smiling. He was obviously pleased with his father's reaction to her plans, but, later, when he brought up the subject of Eleanor, the mood of agreement changed. Adam did not want to believe that his old friend was being difficult, but Chad was insistent.

"Look, Dad," he explained again, and the patience in his voice began to grow on edge. "I know how you feel about Eleanor, but she's got to go. Either I'm going back down to L.A. and fire her, or you're going to find another way to get her out of my hair—at least until after this promotion."

Katherine was rather shocked to see how ruthless Chad could be. He made it quite clear that nothing—not his father, not old loyalties—would be allowed to stand in the way of what he thought was right for Butler's.

The meeting ended and everyone dispersed, going to their rooms to change for dinner. But for Katherine the lingering thoughts of Chad's cold-blooded professionalism would not leave. Did he handle all women the way he was handling Eleanor?

Cocktails were served on the terrace. Katherine had changed into a new emerald silk dress that she had bought the evening before, following Chad's invitation. Since he had shown a preference for green, why should she not wear it? After all, he was keeping his word. Their relationship was "strictly business." So it was only right that she should try to please him a little. She took special care with her hair and makeup too, even going so far as to add some of the glamor touches she had regularly used when she had been a photographers' model. Her efforts were rewarded by the clear looks of approval on the faces of all three men when she walked onto the terrace. Katherine responded with a toss of her red head and a deep laugh of pleasure. She knew how well the silk skimmed her body, hugging each curve in a subtle way that was both provocative and demure.

It was Adam Butler who paid her the most attention, even insisting that she sit next to him at dinner. While he escorted her, he asked a question that had obviously been festering in his mind.

"You are new to Butler's, Katherine, and often it is the newcomer who can see a situation more clearly. Tell me, what do you think of Chad's comments regarding Eleanor?"

Katherine was lost. What could she say that would be both honest and not offensive? Nothing. So her gratitude knew no bounds when Joe interjected and answered for her.

"Adam," he said, "I'll tell you what I think. I think Eleanor is tired. Really tired. You know how hard she works. Why, she hasn't taken a vacation in years—and she's not so young that she doesn't need the rest."

"Umm." Adam was thoughtful. "Thank you, Joe. You may well be right."

Adam was very quiet during dinner. Chad tried to make polite conversation but he, too, seemed preoccupied. It fell to Joe to entertain and that he did, drawling out a string of stories about life in Tennessee. Finally, over coffee, Adam looked up and spoke.

"I've come to a decision about Eleanor."

Katherine saw Chad's eyes narrow.

"Joe has suggested that Eleanor is tired. I think he may be right. She has given her life to Butler's and it shames me to think of how little I have given in return. It's long since time I did something to make her life more rewarding."

Adam was looking at his son and Chad's expression had relaxed. Once again the bond of understanding was there.

"I don't know if you, Chad, or Joe recall my mentioning a special conference the President has asked me to chair, but it begins in Washington next week. It may well be lengthy and, of course, I will be expected to entertain. I think that Eleanor might enjoy attending and acting as my hostess."

Chad said nothing, but from his expression Katherine could tell he was relieved. Perhaps he did not enjoy confrontations as much as she had thought.

Adam rose from the table and they followed him into the drawing room. The dark mood Eleanor had cast was gone and there was a general feeling of elation.

"Chad, you and Joe should take this young lady down to the Beach Club for dancing. Katherine is too young and pretty to spend an entire weekend talking nothing but business."

Katherine started to protest, but Adam would not listen.

"Off you go. I insist. Besides, remember I'm an old man and I need some peace and quiet."

The Del Monte Beach and Tennis Club was situated directly on the sands. When Katherine walked through the door, she became instantly certain that a no more romantic place could exist anywhere.

Chad led them to a table by the windows and seated Katherine so that she faced the splendid view beyond. Lingering fingers of sunlight were spreading across the ocean and in through the glass walls of the clubhouse. Here the panorama was even wider than at Highgates. White sand dunes to their left indicated Carmel and directly across the powerful silhouette of Point Lobos, the magnificent wild sanctuary that was considered the jewel of California's wilderness reserves. To the right, swiftly swallowing the dying sun, was the Pacific, that immense expanse of water that was sending its rythmic beat of waves crashing on the sand and rocks below.

"This is where Rob and I spent all our summers. Here or at the polo field. We didn't take up golf until high school." Chad turned from Katherine to look out into the gathering darkness.

"There were lots of kids here then, and growing up rich was fun. But, of course, the real world comes to everybody whether you're rich or poor. How about a dance?"

He added the last sentence as he rose from his chair and assisted Katherine from hers. Katherine gave Joe a look of apology and followed Chad. His suddenness had disarmed her, and she was too surprised to be nervous of his arms until she was in them.

Dancing with Chad was like being set free from fetters that held her earthbound. Around and around the room they whirled, two bodies melded together and moving as one.

"Did you know that every woman in this room wishes she were as beautiful as you—and every man wishes you were in his arms?" Chad whispered down into her ear.

"You're teasing me again, Chad," she whispered back breathlessly.

"No, I'm not," he insisted. "Just look at the way they're staring."

Katherine obeyed. It was true. Almost every eye was upon them, but she knew the reason for their envy: Chad Butler. Every woman wanted him; every man wanted to be like him. *Yes,* she reminded herself, *every one of these women wants to be in his arms, but I'm the one who is here.* She pressed herself closer, feeling his heart beat against hers, thrilling to the firm touch of his fingers about her waist.

"Let's go outside," Chad whispered urgently. From the sound of his voice she knew that he too was feeling the magic of the moment.

Katherine hesitated, suddenly assailed by fear.

"I—I don't think it would be right."

"Do you care?" he demanded.

"Joe is waiting," she murmured.

He dropped her hand and the set of his mouth hardened. She was safe. It was "strictly business" once more.

"Chad, darling! How are you?" a silvery voice called out from a corner.

Katherine turned and could not believe her eyes. Of all the people in the world! It was like facing the devil in a female guise.

Carole Seeley was smiling her world-famous smile and her white-blond hair gleamed as so many streaks of moonlight against her golden skin. She was exquisite and she was as evil as any woman Katherine had ever known. Tonight it was Carole's choice not to recognize Katherine even though they had worked together for those two unforgettable years in New York.

"Come here, darling. I want you to meet some of my friends." In a twinkle Carole had moved to Chad's side, tucked her hand through his arm, and was guiding him away, leaving Katherine to stand upon the dance floor alone.

The music started and Joe rescued her from embarrassment.

"Wow! Who is she?" Joe asked as they started dancing.

"Don't you recognize Carole Seeley? She's on the cover of at least three magazines every month." Katherine's tone was hardly pleasant, but since she and Joe were eye to eye in height, she managed a tight smile.

"Meow." Joe was not fooled.

"That's not it at all. I just happen to have known her for a long time and she's not very nice."

"Meow, meow."

"Oh, stop it, Joe!" She could no longer contain her temper as she saw Chad take Carole onto the dance floor. Chad should enjoy this embrace, she thought angrily. Carole Seeley's dress left little to the imagination, and Katherine was quite certain that beneath it Carole was naked.

"Take me back to Highgates," she ordered. "I have a dreadful headache."

Joe raised his eyebrows in disbelief. "I'll get the car keys," he said, resigned to Katherine's bad humor.

Katherine walked back to the table and tried to pretend she did not notice the eagerness with which Joe approached Carole and Chad. Her face turned hot with shame as the three stood and talked. Even her ears betrayed her, for she could hear their laughter. After what seemed an eternity, Joe returned.

"Ready?" he asked.

Katherine could not leave fast enough. The drive back to Highgates was silent. When they arrived, Joe walked Katherine to the door and explained how he was returning to join the others.

"Sorry about your headache, Katherine, but that's too good a party to miss."

Katherine said she understood, and she did—all too well.

Joe started to walk back to the car, then turned and stopped.

"Say, how would you like to join our golf game tomorrow?" he asked, as if a golf game could make up for this evening's humiliation.

"No, thanks!" Katherine's words were choked with tears, and as Joe stood there, looking uncertain, she turned from him and closed the door firmly behind her.

CHAPTER SIX

Sounds of men's voices drifted up from the drive below. They awakened Katherine, but for the moment she chose to ignore them and languidly stretched the muscles of her body, experiencing a sensual delight that drew a slow and dreamy smile across her lips. With her eyes still filled with the spell of sleep, she gazed up through the pale dimity canopy and to the yellow field of cornflowers beyond.

How perfect everything was. How much she would like this moment to go on forever. From outside she could hear the low rumble of Chad's laugh. It gave her body a warm feeling all over, and she twisted her head ecstatically into her pillow. She loved the sound of his voice in all of its many moods: giving orders at a business meeting, demanding action from a recalcitrant employee, speaking warmly with his father, and whispering intimacies in her ear, which had sent a thrilling chill coursing through her body the evening before.

Katherine looked over and noted with a secret smile the unused pillow and untouched half of bed beside her. Before she could check the impulse, a tidal wave of desire swept over her, catching her in the dream of Chad's presence beside her . . . his flesh embracing hers . . . his hungry lips searching for the wide vein of fire he had shown her she possessed.

"Fool!" She cried the word at herself as the humiliating implications of her own thoughts threw her from the bed as surely as if it had been charged with an electric current.

"How easily you allow yourself to forget! He abandoned you last night. Yes, abandoned! Left you alone, a mocking joke if Joe hadn't come to your rescue." Katherine covered her face with her hands and felt the anguished tears fall through her fingers as the images of Chad with Carole Seeley filled her mind. She realized that Carole knew every trick in the book—no man could resist her seductive charms. What was more, Katherine's last look of Chad had been of a man who had no intention of resisting. Nonetheless the sounds of the men departing drew her to the window. Carefully she stood to one side from where she could not be seen. Below they were adjusting the cumbersome golf bags into the trunk of a handsome Cadillac roadster.

She could not help but smile when looking at Joe. He was dressed in bright green and yellow, and his almost iridescent appearance made him the perfect pitch man for a soft drink. Adam was already in the car's front seat. She could see the vivid blue of his shirt contrasting with the gleaming white of his hair.

Another man Katherine recognized as having been a part of Carole Seeley's party the previous night. No doubt he was quite attractive, but she could give him no credit for it. Her eyes were on Chad.

He had finished packing the golf clubs and shut the car's trunk with unnecessary firmness. Katherine was lured to lean forward from her hiding place just in time to catch Chad's eyes as he looked boldly up at her. The way in which he brazenly looked at her and allowed his eyes to drift to the sheerness of her negligee made Katherine flush heatedly, and catching a handful of the revealing apricot gown up to her chin, she slipped once more behind the curtain. Here her timidity did battle with her growing curiosity, and curiosity was the easy victor. Again she slipped her face around the curtain's edge.

How awful! Everyone was already in the car and all she could see of Chad was the dark crimson of his shirt through the open sunroof. She watched as his shoulder bent forward, and heard the ignition respond to the turn of his key. The car began to purr forward.

No longer afraid of being seen, Katherine leaned all of the way into the window seat and pressed her nose against the screen. At that moment the car was directly below her, and while Adam and the others joked, Chad slowed the car for just an instant, threw his head back, and looked directly into Katherine's waiting eyes.

There was no expression on his face, no discernible meaning at all. Yet the fire in those dark eyes burned Katherine to her soul. Was he mocking her? She could not know. Then she recalled with irony how just a few days before she had been telling herself how unimportant any of his romantic flings would be so long as they could retain their solid business relationship. Well, once again, she had won a hollow victory. She had rebuffed every one of his romantic overtures and delivered him into the long and practiced arms of Carole Seeley. She should be very proud of herself. Instead she burst into tears.

After blotting her eyes with cold cloths to relieve the telltale puffiness, Katherine crept back to the bed, half hoping to recapture the delectable dreams of earlier. They did not come and she tossed hopelessly, her mind again filled with pictures of Chad and Carole, this time embracing. At last she arose and looked at the tiny jeweled bedside clock. It was only seven thirty. There was plenty of time to bathe before breakfast. She filled the tub until the room was fogged with steam and indulged herself by using every one of the elegant bottles that had been placed there for such occasions: bath crystals, colognes, powders, gels, and masques.

When she emerged and stepped into her dressing room, she found that, unlike Southern California, Carmel knew its seasons. The air from the open window had a decided nip in it. She was glad that she had packed her turquoise sweater set. They had just enough green in their color to enhance her eyes and were a perfect match to her prized heather tweed skirt. Around her neck she hung a heavy chain that held her only heirloom, a gold watch that had belonged to her grandmother. As she brushed her hair and applied a touch of color to her lips, Katherine nodded at her mirrored image with a degree of pleasure. Today, at least in her appearance, she fit in perfectly with the "California Bluebook" set.

The upstairs hall was empty, and Katherine's footsteps down the lengthy staircase fell in silence. She had never much admired Oriental rugs but she had to admit the subtle beauty of these carpets that covered every floor, including the staircase. They were thick and cushiony to the step, yet there was a resiliency that would match the test of time. It was the colors, however, that really caught and held Katherine's fascination. Each one was like a jewel, and the raw light of morning showed them off for what they were.

Katherine found that the entryway and downstairs area were as silent as the upstairs had been, and she wandered into the dining room, hoping to find some company. No one was to be seen, but the room itself was even more impressive than it had been on the previous evening. The soft green damask drapes were pulled fully open, showing

98

the beautifully mullioned window with its intricately traceried triple arch. The satinlike wood of the Adams dining table winked in the pale light, but the lustrous surface was empty except for an enormous arrangement of bronze-colored chrysanthemums and a silver bell, which stood alone.

Each of the inlaid mahogany sideboards was laden with three double-lidded silver serving dishes, while on one board two pitchers offered a choice of fruit juice and on the other board a silver coffee urn and a cozy covered teapot waited. Cups and saucers were available, as were glasses for the juice; but no plates or silverware were present.

Katherine poured a huge glass of orange juice and considered how this sumptuous spread must be quite like those incredible meals that had been served to Henry VIII. It was preposterous that this amount of food could be meant just for her. The men must be returning soon. She would finish her juice and perhaps have a cup of coffee while waiting for them. But the delicious aroma drifting from beneath the covers of the dishes was too much for her to simply ignore. Gingerly she lifted each ivory-handled lid.

"Good heavens!" Katherine exclaimed. "It is a meal for a king." There were sherried chicken livers, kippers in butter and lime, trout, ham, thick sausages, and a dish filled with more bacon than she had ever seen in one place. The last double dish was reserved for pastries and toast, while adjacent to it were placed a galaxy of jam pots. She wondered idly what her old friends from childhood would think of such an array. Then she smiled at the silliness of it; with maybe a sausage or a bit of that bacon they would run right back to the simple fare they knew.

Sipping the juice, she walked to the window. With no one else in sight it was as if all of nature's beauty was meant for her eyes alone. Impulsively she moved over to one of the French doors, unlatched it, and stepped out.

The earlier chill was quickly evaporating and Katherine watched spellbound as the sun's heat drew dew from the terrace stones and turned it into fairy mist.

Standing at the balustrade, she could see an arbor in the near distance at the cliff's edge. A wooden stairway appeared to start from near it and lead to the cove below.

Much as she would have loved to explore the cove, Katherine was certain that the men would be returning before she would have the chance to really enjoy such an adventure. It seemed far more practical to follow the terrace around to her right. In no time she found herself at the drive. Across the smooth tarmac the broad lawn and pond were beckoning irresistibly.

The grass was wet but Katherine did not care. The lure of the bronze boy was too strong. When she reached the pond, she found that, whereas every other area of the estate was carefully manicured, the low-lying ground surrounding the pond had been allowed to remain in its natural state. Reeds and rushes and all manner of native marsh plants lined the shore, in some places for as much as twenty feet. Some of the wild grasses grew so tall that the tunneling of small animals was quite evident. Katherine could imagine small boys tunneling too.

She was nearing the mystical youth, approaching him from his curved and pensive back; and, as she did so, the magic of his spell seemed to catch upon the breeze, creating an alluring tune. Katherine was certain that she could hear, carried upon the air, the musical chatter of happy boys and the tinkling laugh of a beautiful woman. Yet when she actually reached out and touched the cool metal of the figure, the breezes changed and the sound was gone.

Katherine understood why. It was because she did not belong. There was nothing unfriendly here. Quite to the contrary, there was the warm sun, the smell of the marsh, the beauty of the setting. But her childhood was in the past. She had no place among the Lost Boys. Even though she found herself longing to share in their memories, these treasures belonged to another and she was only an intruder. Carefully she edged away, and as she did the breeze returned with its strange, melodious tune.

The incident was haunting, and Katherine began to wonder even more about Chad's mother and brother. What kind of people had they been? How had they died?

Still holding her empty juice glass, she reached the drive and turned toward the side of the terrace where she had not been before. From here could be seen an immense garden, spreading back into the grounds and protected from the whims of the ocean by a strong line of eucalyptus. Katherine had seen photos of flower fields as vast as this, but they had always been those of professional growers. Here were what had to be thousands of plants, primarily chrysanthemums, in every size and shape and color, and at least a half dozen people were busily working between the staked rows.

"Magnificent, isn't it?"

The voice beside Katherine came as such a surprise, she nearly lost hold of her glass.

"I'm sorry. I didn't mean to give you such a fright."

It was Mrs. Chambers, the housekeeper.

"When I have the time, I like to come here and look at the fields too," she continued, less prim and more friendly than at yesterday's meeting. "I know it may seem strange for a house like Highgates to be growing so many flowers, but we give most of them away: to churches, hospitals, and people who just love flowers."

Katherine looked at Mrs. Chambers for what seemed like the first time. Yesterday she had been too overwhelmed to really see this nice, mousy little woman.

Today Mrs. Chambers's round body was dressed in muted blue and her eyes, shining out from friendly crinkles, were the same slate color. Yes, Katherine decided, Mrs. Chambers was a bit of a house mouse, but charmingly so.

Mrs. Chambers did not seem to mind Katherine's scrutiny.

"I see you've had your juice, Miss Dunn. Would you care for the rest of your breakfast now?"

"No, thank you. I thought I'd wait for the men to return."

Mrs. Chambers was clearly surprised. "But, Miss Dunn, the men ate hours ago! They won't be back until late afternoon."

For a mere instant Katherine's face fell, but she caught herself and pasted on a smile. She had not realized how much she had been counting upon Chad's return. Without him the day was really quite empty. From the corner of her eye she saw Mrs. Chambers was watching her with curiosity, and a blush crept into her cheeks.

"You mean that all of the staff has been waiting for me? That all of that food—Oh! I'm so sorry! I saw the food but there were no plates or silverware. It looked to me like you were just getting things ready." The blush had become crimson by now. *This is what happens,* she thought bitterly, *when a girl from the sticks tries to mix with society.*

"Now, now, Miss Dunn, don't be upset," Mrs. Chambers said, patting Katherine's arm. "It's nothing, really. But didn't you see the silver bell waiting on the table?"

"Yes, I saw it, but it didn't mean anything to me."

"Well, my dear"—Mrs. Chambers smiled engagingly—"if you had rung that bell, the kitchen staff would have known to set up for you, and whether to prepare you an omelet or French toast or whatever you would fancy to go with the other dishes."

Katherine was aghast. "Oh, but I couldn't possibly eat

102

all of that food! I mean at home I only have a boiled egg and toast."

"Then there isn't any problem, is there?" Mrs. Chambers said cheerfully, and, taking the juice glass from Katherine's hand, she led the girl around the terrace and back in through the French doors. "Why don't you help yourself to some of that coffee while I make the arrangements."

Katherine looked at the six serving dishes, still simmering over their individual warming candles, and felt overwhelmed with guilt.

"But all of this food will go to waste."

Mrs. Chambers shook her gray curls. "We have too many mouths at Highgates to ever waste food." And with that she flounced her well-rounded self in the direction of the kitchen.

When she returned, Katherine had poured herself the coffee and was admiring the chrysanthemum arrangement on the table.

"These must come from your gardens."

"Oh, yes. We always try to have chrysanthemums about for Mr. Adam. They were Mrs. Butler's favorite. She was born in November and that's the month for mums, you know. She loved every kind of flower, but most especially these. Of course you know it was she who started the gardens."

Katherine sipped her coffee slowly. "Did you know Mrs. Butler well?"

"Pooh! Did I know her well? Only since childhood." Seeing Katherine's look of dismay, Mrs. Chambers explained. "Lucy wasn't always rich. She started out same as me. We grew up in Salinas, where our fathers were farmers. Not that we were the best of friends or anything like that—she was a couple of years ahead of me. When she graduated from high school, she came over to work at the lodge. She was so smart and pretty that they put her

103

on the front desk. Couple of years later when I came, they put me in the kitchen.

"Mr. Adam used to come to the lodge often, and after he'd caught sight of Lucy, he came all of the time. In a year or two they were married, down at the old mission. There's some still say it was the most beautiful wedding ever."

Mrs. Chambers's hands fluttered eagerly as she rambled on with her tale. Katherine was not sure that even wild horses could have stopped the flow of words.

"They went around the world for their honeymoon," she continued. "By the time they returned, I'd married, had one baby and was pregnant with the second. Of course I'd kept working, times being as they were. Lucy and Mr. Adam were living down in Los Angeles, close to the stores. For a while I didn't see much of them. And then came my tragedy."

Katherine looked closely at the little woman and watched her face start to crumple and then stiffen with resolve.

"I lost my family in a fire, Miss Dunn, and if it hadn't been for Lucy Butler, I don't know what would have happened to me. It was her who put arms around me and made me feel human again. I could find no reason to go on until she brought me here. She explained how old Mr. Butler had built Highgates but how he was too infirm to care for it anymore."

Mrs. Chambers closed her eyes and a small smile of pride came onto her face. "I can remember just how she said it. 'Anna, I want you to make this your home. I want you to learn to love it and everything about it. Make it as beautiful as you can.' "

Mrs. Chambers opened her eyes and broadened her smile. "And that's what I've done, Miss Dunn. That's what I've done."

While the kitchen girls had been clearing the sideboards, Katherine and Mrs. Chambers had gradually moved out into the entry. Suddenly Mrs. Chambers asked, "Would you like to see a picture of Lucy Butler?"

It was exactly what Katherine wanted, but still she hesitated. Lucy Butler seemed such an awesome personality that Katherine felt shy and intruding. "I have seen a small photograph," she said rather awkwardly.

"Oh, no! That's not like this. In fact there are two of them. Follow me and I'll show you."

Katherine followed the little woman's busy footsteps down a long hallway and into what was obviously Adam Butler's bedroom. The furnishings were sparse but of fabulous value. Three walls were paneled while the fourth had the same kind of mullioned window as the dining room and offered a similar view.

At the opposite end from the huge antique bed was a comfortable fireside arrangement, and above the mantel was the life-size portrait of a young woman of dazzling beauty. It was not so much the perfection of her features, though they were pleasingly balanced. Nor was it the rich darkness of her hair and eyes that caused this girl's appearance to be so incredibly effective. It was the vitality that emanated from every part of her: the rich warmth of her skin and hair, the twinkle that the artist had captured in her eyes, the air of restrained movement. All of these led to the inescapable feeling that, if she wished, this remarkable young woman could step out of the frame and join the conversation at any moment.

"That was painted on their honeymoon," Mrs. Chambers explained. "Mr. Adam likes it best."

Katherine was quite content to stand before this extraordinary painting and study the subject longer, but Mrs. Chambers had something else to show her. It was another life-size painting and this one hung in Adam Butler's private study.

This painting, however, had obviously been done several years later because the twins were also featured and Katherine judged their age to be about five. The green parkland surrounded them and in the near distance was the pond, but Peter Pan had not yet come. Katherine became so absorbed in this painting that Mrs. Chambers did not even try to move her on.

Lucy Butler was even more beautiful here. She had traded the teasing twinkle and taut excitement of her youth for a richer ripeness, a look of secret knowledge, compassion, and an all-encompassing love that filled the room and touched each person who entered.

The boys caught Katherine's special attention. In the photograph she had seen at Cielo she could not tell one from the other. Here it was obvious. Chad stood to his mother's left. He looked directly out at the viewer, his face without expression, but his eyes and physical manner clearly implied self-knowledge and strength.

Rob stood at his mother's right. He was holding her hand in an affectionate gesture, and about the corners of his mouth were lines of tender sweetness that his brother had never possessed.

Katherine studied the group for several minutes. Her thoughts were totally absorbed by the handsome, strong-willed boy who had become the potent, passionate man; and on his youthful lips, pink and full, which had grown into a mouth that filled her with desire. At last she spoke, murmuring only half aloud. "I always thought that Chad looked exactly like his grandfather, but now, after seeing his mother, I'm not so sure."

"I remember old Mr. Butler clearly, Miss Dunn." Mrs. Chambers nodded her head assuredly. "And those boys were a real mix."

Katherine agreed, but privately she could not forget Lucy Butler's long hands, her fine high cheekbones, and, most of all, her sensual mouth.

Katherine stepped back out into the hall and Mrs. Chambers closed the door behind them. Calmly she led Katherine back toward the dining room. But Katherine's emotions were too raw. After spending half an hour listening to Mrs. Chambers's story, and after seeing the family portraits, she could not simply stop there.

"What happened?" she demanded. All of her shyness was overcome by her need to know.

"What happened?" Mrs. Chambers repeated the question, not seeming to understand what Katherine had meant. "Oh, do you mean what happened to Lucy and Rob?"

"Yes! No one down at the store seems to know." Katherine's words were terse.

Mrs. Chambers stopped their procession and looked into Katherine's face. Her plain features were extremely expressive and right now they were both wise and infinitely sad.

"There isn't any mystery, Miss Dunn. They drowned."

"Drowned!" Katherine gasped. "How?"

"They were sailing. It was a beautiful day, just like this. They both were expert with the riggings. Mr. Adam was in Los Angeles and Chad was away at school. Rob was home recovering from a broken leg he'd gotten playing polo.

"When they left, right after lunch, Lucy said, 'Anna, we'll be back in time for dinner.' And dinner is always at six. When they didn't return, we had everyone for miles looking, but no one found a thing. It was as though they had vanished into the air."

Mrs. Chambers shook her head somberly. "It was days and days before they found their bodies."

Katherine shuddered at the pictures Mrs. Chambers's words presented. How had Chad and Adam gone on living here after such a hideous loss?

"Of course it changed everything. All the laughter and gaiety were gone. Mr. Adam spent all his time in Los Angeles. Chad finished college and went to that awful war in Asia. We were all afraid he wouldn't come back."

Mrs. Chambers led Katherine into the dining room, where a delicate linen place mat and matching napkin had been set with the appropriate silverware. She picked up the bell and shook it briskly. A rosy-cheeked girl emerged from the kitchen carrying a plate that offered a boiled egg, a rasher of bacon, and a freshly baked brioche. Mrs. Chambers herself replenished Katherine's coffee.

"It's been a long time since the accident, Miss Dunn. Sixteen years. The wounds are as healed as they'll ever be."

She seemed ready to leave the room but fussed nervously at needless details. At last she said, "Forgive me, Miss Dunn, for taking up so much of your time with talk. It's not often I have another woman to talk with, other than the serving girls. I'm afraid I took advantage of it."

Katherine gave her a warm smile. "I enjoyed every minute," she said with almost complete candor. "And thank you for arranging this beautiful breakfast."

Mrs. Chambers bobbed her tightly curled head and returned to the kitchen, leaving Katherine to enjoy her meal in peaceful solitude, but with a head filled with seething new ideas.

When she had finished, Katherine picked up the silver bell and gave it a solid jingle. She was glad when it was Mrs. Chambers who responded.

"What time did you say the men would be returning?"

"Sometime between four thirty and five. You have all day to enjoy yourself, miss."

"Thank you, Mrs. Chambers." Already Katherine's thoughts were on the stairway leading to the cove.

Changing into her swimsuit took no time at all. It was new, of course. Like the dress, she had purchased it after Chad's invitation. The adventure at Cielo had taught her to come prepared.

Katherine rubbed sun-screen lotion into her white skin and thought, with a twinge of envy, of Carole Seeley's sultry tan and her own inability to acquire even the faintest brown. There were compensations, however; for instance, the silken texture of her skin was something an avid sunbather like Carole had long ago lost.

She gave herself a brief examination in the mirror. Yes, her choice had been a good one. The deep wine color of the suit played up both her fairness and her coppery hair, while the sleek, uncluttered lines gave pleasing attention to her figure.

Borrowing a bath towel, she slipped into her sandals, picked up the book Joe had asked her to read, and was on her way.

Mrs. Chambers was in the hallway, and when she heard her name called, Katherine feared another lengthy conversation was on its way. Instead the little woman very efficiently removed a key from the large collection she wore tied at her waist and told Katherine to look for beach equipment in the boat house.

The arbor Katherine had seen from the terrace was placed where the view of the cove was best, and next to it was the stairway leading to the beach. It was both long and steep, and as Katherine descended it she counted a hundred and four steps. Climbing back would be good exercise.

The boat house was built of local stone and appeared large enough to store at least four boats. There was a dock running alongside, and Katherine could see the door to which Mrs. Chambers had referred was reached by means of the dock.

Inside it was dark and she could find no lights. Nonetheless it was not difficult to find the beach umbrellas lined up against the wall and stationed next to two shiny paddleboards. Backrests and beach chairs were easy to locate also and in the gloom Katherine could discern the sleek outline of the only boat in residence: a powerful hydrofoil.

Katherine borrowed an umbrella and backrest and was soon comfortably seated, admiring the scenery. The earlier fog had dissipated completely, leaving a cloudless azure sky and the air heavily scented with the varied smells of the sea.

The cove, she guessed, was approximately a quarter of a mile in depth. It was cut into high and rather precipitous cliffs that were liberally crisscrossed by informal paths. The beach, where she sat, was at the farthest end and she rather suspected that its fine white sand had been imported for comfort, because everywhere else the shore was rocky. Above and behind Katherine was the Highgates estate, but on either bluff, at the mouth of the cove, were gently rolling fairways and greens of the Pebble Beach Golf Course. Katherine squinted at a group golfing on the southern bluff, but the figures were not familiar.

Nestling back into the protective shade of the umbrella, she opened the book Joe had urged upon her and, with every good intention, began a study of the economics of advertising. It was a doomed venture. Too many things had been happening in her life for her to sit and quietly ponder the principles of supply and demand as they applied to retail advertising.

Two weeks ago she had grabbed at the chance to come to work at Butler's, and since last Tuesday, when she had stumbled and fallen into the store's handsome president,

Katherine's whole life—her whole way of thinking—had been turned upside down. There were two competing forces: the powerful magnetism of Chad Butler and her own strong-willed determination to be an independent success without ever, in any way, needing a man. Yet now one force threatened to overcome the other.

What was happening? Katherine wondered as she puzzled through her jumbled thoughts. She had always prided herself upon her ability to remain emotionally detached, but Chad Butler was introducing her to a brand-new spectrum of feelings.

Be honest and admit it, she admonished herself. *You want him to make love to you. You felt it at Cielo, no matter what you pretended. You felt it again last night. And if you are not very careful, Chad will see right through your transparent playacting and make the most of your weakness.*

Just thinking about Chad, and the effect his merest touch had upon her senses, had quickened her pulse. Resolutely she turned her thoughts from his dark, sensual powers and once again attempted to concentrate upon Joe's book. It was no use. Sighing deeply, Katherine gave in to the warm sun and closed her eyes.

The quiet lap of the tide lulled her to sleep, but dreams only continued her troubled thoughts. Eleanor Graham wandered through: tough, successful, and lonely. Dee warned of an empty bed. And, finally, Chad appeared, angrily accusing her of being hard and cold.

Out of this turmoil came one quiet picture of reassurance. It was of Lucy Butler, the older Lucy, sitting on the lawn with her boys beside her. Suddenly Katherine knew what the picture had been trying to tell her. Lucy Butler had learned that the secret of life is love.

The thought snapped Katherine awake. Love. Love like Lucy Butler had given and received, even in death. Love like Mrs. Chambers, who could give herself to another family when her own had fallen in ashes. Love like her mother had given to her with each sacrifice and encouragement. And, yes, the love her father had given her, had lavished upon her until its strange end.

A chilling question entered her mind. What kind of love had she given? Precious little.

Katherine leaped up from her towel. It was all too much to deal with at one time. Her mind was more of a muddle than before. A good swim would cure that. She was almost to the water's edge when she remembered the gleaming paddleboards waiting in the boat house.

She chose the red one and quickly launched it and herself from the dock's ladder. The water was much colder than she had expected, and after swimming vigorously and pushing the board on ahead, Katherine climbed aboard and allowed herself to float in the warming sun. The gentle rolling of the tide reminded her of childhood. Maybe it was time to stop hating her father for having deserted her and be grateful for the years of love and joy that he had given to her.

Katherine was now well past the middle of the cove, and looking up, she saw a group of figures on the northern bluff. It was Chad and the others. With strong, broad strokes Katherine pulled the board toward the mouth of the cove, and when she reached a place from which she thought she could be heard, she began to call up to the golfers, but no one responded. Katherine pulled the board a little further and called up again. She was on the verge of giving up when Chad heard her. He ran to the cliff's edge and yelled down to her. A swift wind from outside the cove lifted his words and carried them away. Katherine smiled and waved, pleased at his attention.

By now Katherine was in the mouth of the cove. She found the wind chilling and the current far stronger than she had anticipated, but still she was enjoying her voyage enormously. The water was her friend, and if she tired, the northern coastline was close at hand.

Not more than a hundred yards beyond the cove's mouth stood the first of three jagged rock islands. They were home for thousands of seabirds, primarily cormorants but with a few pelicans and a growing number of sea lions. Each of the rock islands had a name. Chad had pointed them out last night, but she had not remembered. Now she floated on the tide, watching the blackbirds swoop madly from the sky and unerringly snap up their squirming prey in sharp beaks.

Katherine began to note that the water was moving in stronger, faster, even crisscrossing currents as it rose and surged between the rocks. And when she caught the eye of a lounging sea lion, who regarded her dourly and then slipped off his perch and into the sea, she knew it was time to turn for the shore. She started to turn the board around but found that her shoulder muscles had tightened from the cold. The fact that the board refused to respond to her efforts was even more disturbing.

She was not yet frightened, but as the sea pulled her closer and closer to the rocks, Katherine recognized just how quickly her strength was failing. The cold of the water and her overlong exposure to it were taking their toll. Even her legs were giving her ominous signs of cramping. For the moment all that she could hope for was to stay afloat. In an instant even this was denied, as from somewhere far below a dynamic force emerged, tossing both Katherine and the board as though they were flecks of foam. Momentarily she was dazed and then, feeling her lungs cry out for air, she realized that she was trapped beneath the board as the broad body of the sea lion swam oppressively near. She refused to panic, and forcing herself to the edge of her dwindling energy, she shoved the board aside and pulled her body partially on top.

113

Always she had thought of the water as her friend; now, in the space of seconds, it had become her deadly enemy. The currents would not let her rest. They pulled her from the board one last time. She was their plaything now, a bit of flotsam to be dragged down into the ocean's churning depths then hurled to the surface, where she would take a desperate gasp of life-giving air. At one such interval she caught a blurry glimpse of the men on the cliff all gesturing wildly and she thought she heard someone calling "Over there . . . Chad! Over there!"

It had to end. She knew that it did. There was not much life left in her. She was between the rocks now and her only chance was to somehow grab hold and pull herself out of the water. As though the sea knew it might be robbed of this new plaything, it swept up in a powerful wave that sucked Katherine to its bosom and then spat her out against the rock so that she struck her head and slid limply down into the ocean's implacable folds.

Katherine found herself in a dark and peaceful cavern and as she drifted further into the dark she decided it was a very pleasant place to be until, from somewhere outside her own body, a hot and violent force of air pushed into her lungs and stayed there until her lungs, of their own accord, pushed the air back out and the whole process began all over. With the greatest effort Katherine opened her eyes, but she could not see. Someone's hand was over the upper half of her face, pinching closed her nostrils while this strange and painful procedure repeated itself again and again. Why didn't they leave her alone? It was restful where she had been. She wanted to return, but this force would not let her.

Gradually, as her mind revived, Katherine realized there was a pattern: violent action, peace; violence, peace. At last she managed to open her eyes during one of the peaceful interludes and saw that the face just above hers,

114

its eyes wild with untold emotion, was Chad Butler's. Swiftly his hand came down again, tilting her head back, pinching her nostrils, while his mouth embraced hers in a powerful vacuum. Again the hot gust of life poured out of Chad's body and filled Katherine's, and she knew that somehow he had saved her.

When she could breathe easily, Chad sat back, his broad chest heaving from the effort. He watched Katherine keenly as her natural vigor began to return.

"Just relax," he panted. "Dad's bringing up the boat, but it might take a while."

Katherine's eyes scanned the tiny rock-edged cove where Chad had brought her. They seemed to be totally isolated from the rest of the world. She had only to look into Chad's eyes to confirm her vulnerability. Frightened of herself as well as him, Katherine tried desperately to sit up, only to be overwhelmed with dizziness and a sudden attack of the chills.

"Stay put!" Chad commanded, thrusting her shoulders back toward the sand. At his touch she began shaking violently, and Chad quickly wrapped her in his arms, lowering himself beside her so that he could intertwine his body with hers and share his physical warmth.

"You are so cold, so terribly cold," he whispered tenderly, and Katherine could feel the heat of his breath through the tangled mat of her wet hair. His voice was charged with emotion, and then, sighing deeply, he seemed to relax. Yet Katherine could still feel the beat of his heart, like an iron ball, against her breast.

"Thank God you're alive," he groaned, pressing her closer. "If I had lost you too . . ."

Katherine tried to speak, but her words were drowned as Chad's warm, expressive mouth once again encompassed her own, this time in a lingering kiss as gentle as a sweet caress. Katherine's heart fluttered violently. In a blinding instant the lassitude that had filled her fell before an invasion of emotion that quickly swept her into a wild wave of desire. It was the tip of her tongue that issued the first invitation.

Chad backed away, smiling slyly.

"Oh, you are delicious," he murmured as his dark eyes, burning with a raw light, slowly examined the length of her body.

A new boldness, born in the heat of need, consumed Katherine. Wordlessly she reached for Chad, coiling her long arms about his neck and pulling him close to her once more.

As their bodies touched she became dizzily aware of the bristling texture of Chad's broad chest tantalizing the sensitive flesh of her breasts.

Chad answered the question in her eyes.

"I'm afraid there isn't much left of your swimsuit. It must have caught on one of the rocks."

Instead of stiffening with embarrassment and fear, Katherine relaxed and smiled dreamily as she lifted her lips to meet Chad's. Fate had intervened, leaving her completely vulnerable to the man she loved. What would happen was inevitable, a part of the law of nature—a marvelous, marvelous part. Closing her eyes, she surrendered to the roaring, all-consuming fire of passion that promised to engulf them.

Chad's mouth followed the path of his insistent hands across her shoulders, roving hungrily over her breasts, down the silken skin beyond her waist until, at last, his fingers freed her from the last constraints of the shredded swimsuit. And Katherine responded in kind. A woman possessed by love and her lover, she answered Chad's every caress, every kiss, every touch with those of her own. Desire to please. Desire to have. Desire.

Her eyes were closed and she was astride the cresting

tide of flame when Chad broke from their embrace. Katherine lifted her empty arms, reaching for him and pleading softly for his return.

"Patience, my gorgeous Kate," he answered huskily, and opening her eyes, she saw a bronze giant standing beside her, every inch of him as magnificent as the lusty gods of Greece.

Swiftly Chad gathered her to himself and locked her in an embrace that knew no end but ecstasy.

Later, much, much later, Katherine awoke. Somehow she was back in the canopied bed, only now the blue cornflowers were leaping away from the yellow walls and threatening to smother her. Besides this illusion Katherine found that her head was aching and she was desperately thirsty.

"Drink this," Mrs. Chambers was saying helpfully as she lifted a warm spoon to Katherine's dry lips. "You've been sleeping more than six hours now. A little of this broth is what you want. Mr. Parkman, will you be so kind as to help me here?"

Joe stepped out of the shadows and gently held Katherine while Mrs. Chambers coaxed the nourishing liquid between the drowsy girl's lips. Halfway through, Katherine shook her head. She did not want any more. Even Mrs. Chambers's reasoning that the broth would give her strength was not enough to induce a change of mind.

"Where's Chad?" she asked feebly.

"He just left to take Carole home," Joe told her.

Katherine stiffened.

"I had no idea that you and Carole knew each other so well," he continued. "Why, she absolutely refused to leave until Chad could assure her that you were all right."

Katherine closed her eyes, thinking of clever, scheming

117

Carole Seeley and how she would like to strangle Joe for his naiveté.

Joe seemed to think that she was falling back to sleep and began to lower her onto the pillows, but not before giving her a mild reproof for her comments of the previous evening.

"You know, Katherine, I don't think you have been giving Carole a fair chance. She really cares for you."

This time his words were more than Katherine could stand. "Mrs. Chambers," she called in a soft but unwavering voice. "I think I'd better have more of that soup."

If chicken soup would give her strength, then Katherine was prepared to drink gallons of it. Anything to ensure her ability to fly out of Carmel in the morning, making sure first that Chad flew with her.

Undoubtedly she was being a fool, but Katherine was not ready to give Chad up to Carole yet. When the room was empty and she was alone, waves of anxiety washed over her as all of the details of what had happened between her and Chad flooded her memory, kindling twin emotions of desire and humiliation.

Her surrender to Chad had been as genuine as it had been complete. She had wanted his lovemaking and she had been as eager to give to him as she had been to receive—from his lips, his tongue, his hands, his entire being—the endless sensations that mounted one upon another until they had combined to lead her out of herself and into a realm where there was only feeling.

The tiny spasm of pain had been a surprise, but it was as nothing when compared to the long, golden possession they had shared so ecstatically. Yet, when at last it was over, Chad had spoken words that had cut to the core of her soul.

"I'm sorry," he had told her in a rough and urgent voice. "I had no idea."

118

"Sorry?" She had been bewildered and still innocent.

"Why didn't you tell me?" he demanded, and suddenly his tone was edged with anger.

"Tell you what?"

"Why from the way you—" He paused awkwardly and, standing up, reached for his clothes in a manner that made Katherine want to hide from her own nakedness.

Chad turned back to look down upon her. All the passion that had fired his eyes was gone, as though, for him, the moment had never existed.

"If you had told me," he said coldly, "well, I never would have allowed myself to be the first."

Katherine clutched her arms about herself and tried to turn from his peering eyes. How could he turn her gift into such an ugly thing?

Chad knelt beside her and Katherine felt the roughness of his fingers upon her shoulder—the same fingers that only moments before had lifted her into a questing state of desire.

"Katherine, I'm sorry. I didn't mean to hurt you."

His words lashed at her relentlessly, and as the sound of a powerful motor became more and more evident, hot tears spilled silently down Katherine's cheeks.

Chad hailed the hydrofoil, and when it pulled abreast of their rock-edged hideaway, he called for a blanket, then tossed it carelessly to Katherine, who huddled herself miserably in its warm protection.

To add insult to injury, Carole Seeley was at the boat house to greet them. Somehow she had made herself a part of the golfing party. As always Carole was sleek and glamorous, and the look she gave to Katherine was one of sheer contempt.

Humiliated beyond endurance, Katherine gave in to an overwhelming weakness and permitted the men to carry her up the steep staircase in an old beach hammock. There

Mrs. Chambers greeted them and Katherine gratefully submitted to the housekeeper's care. The last thoughts she had before drifting into a deep and dreamless sleep were of Chad and the cruel reality that what he had wanted was not the self-consuming, all-giving love that she had offered with such free abandon. No. All that he had wanted was the practiced touch of a seasoned expert.

CHAPTER SEVEN

The flight back from Carmel was mercifully uneventful, even though it started ominously with Joe's teasing.

"What culture is it," he asked in his drawl, "that says if you save a person's life that person becomes your property?"

"Joe! You're just making that up," Katherine protested a bit too vehemently. Had Joe guessed what had occurred between Chad and her? Or, far worse, was Chad one of those dreadful men who bragged of their conquests? She threw him a sidelong glance and saw the grimly serious expression on his face. No, no. Chad might not return the passion of her feelings for him, but he was not capable of such a despicable act.

Suddenly Chad's voice blurted out in a growl. "Do you realize how near Katherine was to drowning, Joe? Coming that close to death is no joke." His sharp, hard words had the effect of nailing Joe to his seat. Even Katherine, who by now was well aware of the gamut of Chad's emotions, was taken aback by the supressed violence that was here revealed.

Chad was studying his hands as he repeatedly clenched his fists.

"I was damned lucky to get to her in time. The water between those rocks is a death trap. In fact"—he paused to glare at Joe—"it was there, just beyond where Katherine was, that my mother and brother *did* drown."

There was a heavy silence. Joe shifted positions uncomfortably. "Sorry," he said at last. "I didn't know. You're right, it was a lousy thing to joke about." He took a long pull on his pipe and after mouthing a series of smoky rings, he lightened the mood by adding a wry comment. "Guess what folks say about me is true. You just can't take the yokel out of the hillbilly."

Katherine was looking at Chad with new understanding. So that was where it had happened. That was where Lucy and Rob had died, and Chad had braved those very waters to save her from the same fate.

She went on watching him in silence, noting the rows of ugly scratches beneath the dark hair of his arms. Mrs. Chambers had told her how Chad had rushed down the bramble-covered cliff to reach the cove, and these scratches were evidence of his efforts. Katherine's memory was unclear regarding what had happened in the water, but she had relived each detail of the events that followed at least a thousand times in the past few hours. Chad had saved her life and he had made her his possession so completely that she would never be able to give herself to another man. Yet, from his manner, those moments of shared intimacy were completely forgotten. He had hardly spoken to her since those last moments before the boat had arrived, and the cool, formal tone his few words had taken told her clearly that she, too, was to forget the incident.

Abruptly Katherine turned her head to face a window. Forget the most marvelous, most searing experience of her life? She could never forget, but pride and self-discipline

122

would protect her from being a fool. She would pretend to have forgotten. It was the only choice left to her. Chad had seen to that.

When they reached Butler's it was to find that Eleanor had already gone and Dee, efficient as always, had smoothly taken her place.

"Are you sure I can't tempt you back after your baby is born?" Chad asked during lunch one day.

It had become a frequent occurrence for Chad to join Dee's and Katherine's table, and whenever he did so, it was to seek Dee's advice. Katherine he treated so casually that all gossip had died.

Dee answered Chad's question firmly. "No, but thanks. I'm flattered that you'd want me back, but beyond Peter, this little one is going to be the most important person in my world. And when his or her siblings arrive, I want that world to be a happy, snug, secure place."

"Dee, you are crazy to give up the opportunity Chad is suggesting," Katherine interjected. "Why can't you manage to do both? After all, you've worked for years to get where you are. I can't imagine throwing it all away just for a baby."

She knew that her tone had been rather sarcastic, but when she saw Chad's look of disapproval, Katherine tossed her head back and thrust out her chin in defiance. She was annoyed with them both. The way they were always conferring and leaving her out. It was as though they thought the only area of the business she could comprehend was The China Line. It had become infuriating to see the way in which Chad regularly seemed to seek Dee's opinion, but when it came to Katherine he only issued orders.

Katherine eyed her luncheon companions balefully, but Dee remained patient.

123

"This is simply my choice. I don't say it's right for everyone. Lots of women combine careers beautifully, and others, like you, Katherine, only want the business side of it. But for me, Peter and this baby will fill my life quite nicely."

Chad sat back in his chair and looked at her thoughtfully. "I hate to admit it, Dee, because I'm losing a mighty fine publicist, but you're making the right decision."

Katherine felt the slight. Their inference was as clear as it was archaic. The position that Dee had left to her—one she was no longer sure she wanted—made her somehow appear as a lesser kind of woman. While Dee, sitting there in her navy-blue maternity dress, was as righteous and sacred as an Earth Mother goddess. Pushing her chair back, Katherine stood to leave.

"Motherhood and apple pie! The two of you really want to rub my nose in it, don't you?" As soon as she had blurted out her frustration she knew her mistake, and the crippled look on Dee's face only served to underline it.

"Dee," she implored, reaching for her friend's hand. "That was an awful thing t—"

Chad interrupted. "Why apologize? It just goes to show that you're growing more like Eleanor every day." He shook his head with disgust. "What a waste!"

The remainder of the day Katherine spent in the layout department, working with two staff members who were assisting with The China Line promotion.

She found concentration difficult. Her mind insisted on drifting back over Chad's words again and again. No, he had it all wrong. She wasn't going to be like Eleanor Graham. True, she wanted Eleanor's job someday, but not her way of life. "Well, then," an inner voice asked, "what kind of life are you going to have?"

Just before closing time Chad summoned her to his office and broke his news.

"I'm leaving for Shanghai and Beijing tomorrow."

Katherine was so stunned, it was hard for her to follow what he was saying. Leaving? She felt a desperate emptiness creep into her soul.

Chad was explaining that although Karen Su-Chan's daily cables were keeping him informed, he wanted to see the situation for himself.

"Besides," he went on, assessing her coolly, "that puts you in charge—something that will, no doubt, bring you great pleasure. But I'm not worried, you're more than up to it. In fact I think you can handle just about anything, except—" His eyes burned into hers and Katherine braced herself for whatever he was about to say, but instead of pursuing his advantage, Chad swung his chair so that he was facing one of the tall windows.

"Katherine Dunn, you're an enigma. Not a flesh and blood woman, an engima. But,"—he swung his chair back—"you're damn good at your job!"

Katherine stared back at him, her heart in her throat. How long she had worked for this kind of praise and now how meaningless she realized it to be when compared to the hungry needs of her heart.

"How long will you be gone?" she asked numbly, hoping against hope that he would say it was only for a day or two.

"About three weeks."

"But that's when we're scheduled for photography," Katherine protested. He was leaving! She would not see him or hear his voice for three weeks. She felt empty inside.

Chad came across the room and took her hands in his. "Don't worry." He smiled, misreading her anxiety. "I'll be back in time. What's more, I'll bring the caftans and the jewelry you need for photography back with me.

"By the way." He let go of her hands and stepped back

behind his desk. "Joe and I selected our model, and she's someone you know."

Katherine's heart sank. "Who?" she asked tremulously.

"Jessica Spencer. It was a difficult choice, but she's a highly popular model and both Joe and I think that kind of identification will be helpful."

They had not picked Carole Seeley! Katherine felt an incredible relief. All along she had feared they would select the lissome blonde, who, in truth, was a far more sought-after model than Jessica Spencer.

Their conversation drifted on until there was really nothing more to say except good-bye.

Chad was still standing behind his desk and the look in his eyes, as their moment of parting neared, changed to that fathomless, unreadable expression Katherine was learning to know so well. It told her nothing but drew her into itself like a moth to a flame.

She came closer, so that only the desk held them physically apart, yet it might have been a chasm as broad as time.

How can it be this way? she wanted to shout at him. *Aren't you the man who gave me back my life? Haven't we shared at least one moment of real passion? How, then, can it be, when you are leaving me, that all we have to offer one another is a handshake and one empty word—good-bye?*

But it was all, and afterward Katherine left quickly. She made her way back to her own desk and, thankful to be alone, stared with tear-filled eyes out into the gathering darkness.

Time is said to heal all wounds, but during that first week of Chad's absence Katherine found there was an overwhelming void in her life. Dee tried in every way to improve her friend's dismal temperament, and if she guessed the reason for its being, she had the good sense to say nothing.

Joe Parkman was around almost constantly. As The China Line's promotional opening date neared, Joe was dividing his time in three ways: his agency; the various publication, television, and radio people involved; and the source of the promotion's creative ideas, Katherine Dunn at Butler's.

Joe's good humor and solid down-to-earth approach helped to boost Katherine's morale greatly. More and more she found herself looking forward to his visits, and when, one morning, he called and suggested dinner, she was eager to accept.

"Wear something slinky," he requested and then in his typical style added, "I'll do the same. Tonight, for once, we're not going to talk shop."

Katherine laughed and looked forward to an evening of Joe's special brand of humor. Tonight he would have a very appreciative audience.

She took her time in dressing, just as Joe had asked. After a luxurious soak in one of her favorite milk baths, Katherine slipped into the emerald silk she had worn in Carmel. Then, using every glamor trick she had learned as part of a model's primer, she subtly fashioned her facial features so that her green eyes glowed even more dramatically and her lips glistened with invitation. She even pulled her thick hair on top of her head, wrapping and braiding it into an exotic style that gave provocative emphasis to her graceful neck.

Joe made it clear how much he appreciated her appearance by giving her a low wolf whistle when he entered her door. A bit later when he was helping Katherine on with her coat she could tell that he had surveyed her living arrangements critically and was surprised by their frugality.

The restaurant he had chosen was entirely different from anything Katherine had expected. Bright lights and loud music, that was Joe. Tonight, however, he fooled her completely by selecting a discreet little place that specialized in food of Provence, flickering candlelight and a strolling violinist with the soul of a gypsy. It was a place for intimate conversations, hand-holding, whispered words of love. It made Katherine feel quite uneasy.

Her unease grew as over drinks and well into an excellent dinner she waited for Joe to launch into one of his famously funny dialect stories. Instead he remained silent and preoccupied, studying his wineglass and only picking indifferently at his dinner.

"Katherine, I've been thinking about us," he said at last. "How well we get on. The way our minds work together. You know it's not often in our business you find someone whose ideas really ring right along with your own."

What was he getting at? she wondered and took one last bite of the delicious ratatouille.

Joe refilled their wineglasses. "Have I ever told you how I want to open my own agency?"

Katherine shook her head.

"Well, I've been planning on it for years. First I needed the right ingredients: several solid clients I could count upon coming with me, the cash to invest in setting up my own shop, and a partner I could communicate with as well as trust without question."

Through the candle flame Katherine was watching him, and as his meaning began to become clear she slowly placed her knife and fork upon her plate. His words were so surprising that she felt as though she needed to grip the table to maintain a hold on reality.

"I've had the clients and the money for some time. It's

128

the partner that's been hard to find. But every since we met I've had this feeling about you. . . ."

She could scarcely believe it. Joe Parkman was going to ask her to be his partner! Joe, whose reputation virtually ensured success, and not just mediocre success but the blazing neon lights kind she had always dreamed of.

"You know what I'm asking, don't you? I can read it in those gorgeous green eyes." Joe reached across the table and covered one of her hands with his own. "There's no limit to the future we can build."

Katherine felt her pulse racing. She needed quiet and time to think, yet she wanted him to know exactly how flattered she was. "Joe, you're making me the offer of a lifetime. . . ."

"Not *of* a lifetime," Joe interrupted, "*for* a lifetime. I'm asking you to join me in a full partnership, Katherine, as Mrs. Joe Parkman."

Marriage! Marriage to Joe? Such an idea had never occurred to her. Unaware of her own action, Katherine withdrew her hand from beneath Joe's and placed it safely in her lap.

"I can see I've surprised you." Joe was putting a little too much heartiness into his voice. "Take all the time you want. I'm in no hurry for an answer." Suddenly he leaned across the table, his eyes urgent. "I'm not good at romantic talk, Katherine. Maybe you could teach me. But I can promise you I'd make you a good husband."

"What about Carole Seeley? You seemed rather smitten with her when we were in Carmel." Katherine was rashly grabbing at anything in order to give herself time. What was she going to do? She did not want to discuss marriage with Joe, or even think about it. The whole thing was impossible, like a bad dream.

"Carole Seeley is the kind of woman who cultivates that sort of reaction. Believe me, it doesn't last."

129

Not with you perhaps, Katherine thought, *but what about Chad?*

"Is there someone else?" Joe asked suddenly. "Another man?"

Katherine jerked back in surprise. It took her a moment too long to regain her composure. "No, no, no!" she exclaimed emphatically. "There's no other man. Who could there possibly be?"

"Chad," Joe said flatly.

Katherine started to protest, but Joe stopped her.

"You protest too loudly, my dear. I can read the symptoms. I should have seen them all along." He sat back in his chair and looked across at Katherine with a hint of bitterness.

"Chad Butler, the handsome millionaire tycoon. Pretty stiff competition for a hillbilly from Tennessee. I thought you were too smart to fall for all of that razzle-dazzle. Can't you see? You and I come from the same place—nowhere—and we want to get up and out of there. Chad can't understand you. Not like I can. He was born rich. He doesn't know what it's like living in one room with only a hot plate."

"Please, Joe," Katherine pleaded. She had to make him stop. The talk had gone too far. "No more."

Joe pulled out his pipe and began the lengthy process of lighting it. He was giving her ample time for a rebuttal.

"You're right when you say you surprised me." She was trying to pick her words carefully. "No one had ever made me an offer like that before, and really, I wish I could accept because I like you a lot—really I do." She shook her head. The words were tumbling out awkwardly, not at all the way she wanted. "Marriage just isn't in my plans, that's all. I've seen them go sour and I don't want any part of that kind of thing."

Across the table Joe was doing his best to take her

130

rejection well. Katherine's heart went out to him and she gave him a tender smile. "Thank you, kind sir," she said gently, "for the dinner and the most flattering offer a girl could receive. I'm just sorry that I'm the wrong partner."

After that, by silent agreement, the conversation centered upon The China Line. It was enough to keep them going for what remained of the evening.

Much later Katherine found falling asleep next to impossible as she recalled all of what Joe had said, the question he had raised. Was she in love with Chad? Of course she was. Her facade of cool disinterest was just that—a false front with which she fooled the world and even herself until she went to bed at night. Katherine rolled over and pressed the length of her body into the sheets. Chad had given her a rich taste of sensuality and now every inch of her being craved more.

The telephone's ring interrupted a series of wild dreams, and Katherine groped through the dark to reach it.

"You sleep like Rip Van Winkle," a voice said testily. "Do you realize I've already had one contraction since I dialed your number? I've got to get to the hospital before it's too late!"

"Is that you, Dee?" Katherine asked through a sleepy haze.

"Of course it's me. I just wanted to let you know that the Butler's job is all yours."

"Wha—what do you mean?"

"Only that this baby definitely has a mind of its own. It's not due for another three weeks—Ooh! Here comes another pain. Good-bye, Katherine, and good luck!"

It was not until Dee had dropped the phone that Katherine fully understood what was happening. The Cummings baby was arriving early, and she was, by process of elimination, Butler's chief publicist!

Sleep now was impossible, and the few remaining hours

131

until dawn Katherine spent gazing into the darkness, her heart pounding within her breast.

Bless Dee and bless that baby! They were providing her with the answer to her dreams. Joe's idea of an agency was exciting, but, for her, this was much better. There were eleven stores in the Butler chain and she would be planning the publicity for all of them!

Others might have been daunted by such sudden responsibility, not Katherine. And as she lay there in those quiet predawn hours her confidence grew with each passing minute. She could do it, and when Eleanor returned the proof would be so obvious that even that old curmudgeon would have to agree.

Katherine spent the next two weeks moving like a whirlwind. She toured each of the ten Butler branch stores: introducing herself to the various staffs, listening to their ideas, taking note of their problems. It was a winning effort. Everywhere she was met with eager acceptance and full cooperation. Meanwhile she kept Publicity running exactly as Eleanor had instructed and quickly found that with the use of a little charm and several appropriate pats on the back she could make the department more productive than ever before. She found it necessary to stay after hours on a regular basis. It was the best time for creative thinking. Each night she would return to her apartment exhausted but happy in the knowledge that the day had been a private victory.

All of this frenzied activity enabled Katherine to keep thoughts of Chad Butler largely out of her mind during the long hours of the days. Yet every night, when she turned out the lights and crawled into her lonely bed, the same nagging questions and physical cravings assailed her once again.

Gradually she came to understand the permanence of

her feelings, and a chance remark served to underscore it all.

It was three days before Chad was due to return and Mr. Baldwin, a member of the Board, had just completed one of his frequent office visits.

"Miss Dunn," he said respectfully, "I am truly impressed with your efficiency. Why, everything is running so smoothly that Chad and Eleanor could stay away forever."

Katherine was checking the layout for a newspaper ad, and although smiling and nodding politely, she had not really been attentive until three of Mr. Baldwin's words pierced her concentration with a sickening force: Chad . . . away . . . forever. The layout fell from her fingers and she sat pale and trembling, her eyes seeing only the horrible possibilities those three words presented.

Not to see Chad ever again? Not to ever hear his voice or hope to feel the warm strength of his arms and the thrill of his kiss? Not to be able to tell him, to show him in a million private ways, how important he was to her and to her happiness? It was a devastating insight and it forced her to see exactly what she had been hiding from herself.

There was no turning back. She knew it. In a crash the walls of Katherine's fortress of self-reliance toppled forever, and she was left vulnerable as a schoolgirl.

Eagerly Katherine looked up. She wanted to tell Mr. Baldwin, and reassure herself, that Chad was coming home, but the room was empty. The old man had gone.

CHAPTER EIGHT

Just two days remained before Chad's return and they might well have dragged endlessly had it not been for The China Line's demanding photography schedule.

They would shoot the photos Friday at Cielo, and since Chad was arriving Thursday with both the gowns and the jewelry, there was really no flexibility in the timing. It was up to Katherine to make certain everything ran smoothly, and there were so many details to consider that she was left with neither time nor energy to think about her personal life.

Jessica Spencer arrived from New York. She and Katherine spent hours studying designer sketches of the silk caftans and jade jewelry that were to be modeled. Normally the gowns would be on hand, ready for fittings, but in this case Jessica's measurements had been sent to Karen Su and the caftans had been cut to fit in China. Jessica was troubled by this irregularity, and Katherine spent more than a little time soothing her doubts.

"There's nothing for you to worry about," Katherine said, repeating herself for the third time. "Trust Karen Su

134

to make sure that every stitch is properly placed. All you have to do is step into them and smile for the cameras."

"I'm sorry, Katherine, but this funny feeling I have— that something will go wrong—it just won't go away." Jessica shook her sleek, honey-colored hair and it rippled in shining waves.

Katherine looked at her with sympathy. She disliked seeing such concern in those beautiful China Doll eyes. Jessica was one of those rarities in the profession: a perennial sweetheart; as gentle, kind, and loving as she was exquisite. Katherine also knew her to be a perfectionist who insisted on studying every detail of an assignment. Hence it should not have come as such a surprise when, on Wednesday, Jessica announced she wanted to visit Cielo. Katherine balked. She had no time to take Jessica on a tour.

"But I always check locations," Jessica explained reasonably. "There must be someone who can take me."

Katherine frowned and Jessica responded with an expression of tender compassion that could easily melt a stone. Who would be the right person to escort her? Katherine wondered. Joe Parkman was the obvious choice, but she hated to ask him for a favor, and besides, how would he react to such a request?

As if a gesture on her part could ease Katherine's troubled thoughts, Jessica offered her friend a winning, dreamy-eyed smile.

Of course! Of course! Katherine marveled that she had not realized the obvious before. Sending Jessica an exultant grin, she lifted the phone and began to dial. Jessica Spencer was going to be the perfect medicine for Joe's wounded ego.

When Thursday dawned, Katherine found the mounting tension was threatening to gnaw a hole in her stomach. In just twenty-four hours she would be supervising the photography of an investment valued at nearly two million dollars. If things went as they should, The China Line could easily gross more than five times that amount, giving Butler's a net profit that even the most skeptical of the stockholders would approve, and Chad would have the marketing bonanza he wanted. More and more, as the days went by, Katherine was coming to realize that giving Chad what he wanted had become the most important thing in her life.

Upon reaching the office and reviewing the mountainous stack of last-minute phone calls and scheduling problems that demanded her attention, Katherine's nerves were frayed. But she could calm herself with the knowledge that all of the real work had long since been completed and approved.

Chad had personally okayed the layouts, copy, headings, mailers, the three one-minute TV spots, and the series of radio teasers. He had also selected the exact photography locations and had left Katherine with detailed instructions of how they were to be set up. It had been Joe's job to contract with the various media for the specific space and times Chad wanted and to make all of the photography and filming arrangements.

All of this preparation meant that on the day of actual photography everyone involved would be going through their prearranged paces and Katherine's job would be to shepherd the merchandise and the model who wore it, making certain that no detail went unnoticed.

Katherine sipped a cup of coffee and began to attack her list of chores. With everything so well organized what could possibly go wrong? Still her stomach churned, and when Joe arrived to meet Jessica, his reaction provided Katherine with a much-needed chuckle. Joe took one look at Jessica's perfectly proportioned figure, her huge soulful eyes, the long drift of silky hair, and he was lost. Lost, too,

136

it appeared, were any romantic notions about Katherine. Joe's new infatuation was so complete that when he hurried Jessica out of the door only Jessica remembered to say good-bye. Katherine smiled, amused and relieved. Perhaps now her relationship with Joe could return to a more comfortable norm.

The activity of the day ran at a frantic pace, yet Katherine's senses were not completely absorbed by the needs of The China Line. Each ring of her phone, each tap on her door and Katherine's heart throbbed with excited hope. Was it Chad? It never was. By seven thirty her hope was dead. There was no use in hanging around any longer. His flight had been due in hours before. Chad was not going to call.

Briskly she began to pack the things she would be needing at Cielo. There was a melancholy silence about Butler's, as if the walls, the floors, the ceilings, all knew of her hurt and sympathized.

How much she had looked forward to Chad's return! A large tear edged down her cheek as she wondered where he was at that moment and whose arms he would seek for the night.

"That's what you get for thinking he had any interest in you!" she told herself mercilessly and wiped at her eyes with impatience.

Gathering up her things, Katherine walked out and had almost reached the end of the hall when the ringing of a phone caught her ear.

"Don't hang up! Don't hang up!" she cried, dropping everything and running the distance back to her desk.

"Hello? Is that you, Katherine?" Chad's wonderfully deep voice asked anxiously.

"Yes," she answered, breathless. Her heart was choking the voice out of her throat.

137

"My plane was hours late. I never thought I'd catch you."

"Where are you now?" she asked and wondered if he could hear her tears of relief.

"At the town house, and I thought—well, if it's all right with you—I'd send my driver to bring you back here."

"Of course it's all right!" Katherine answered joyously. "I can hardly wait to see what you've brought back."

"I thought you might like to see me," Chad responded, and Katherine could not tell from the tone of his voice if he were teasing or serious.

"Well, that too." She shocked herself with the degree of her understatement.

"You certainly don't do much for a man's ego," Chad added laconically.

"I always thought yours was in good enough shape," Katherine laughed, enjoying the repartee. Everything was going to be all right now. Chad was home and he wanted her!

"I must be crazy, inviting a sharp-tongued career woman to dinner," said the voice at the other end of the conversation. Again Katherine could not be sure whether or not Chad was serious, but his tone was enough to jolt her confidence.

"Don't move," he ordered. "I'll have the car there in twenty minutes."

"I'll be waiting," Katherine promised.

Long after Chad had hung up, Katherine held the phone close to her lips, dreaming wild thoughts of what might soon come. She was still dreaming when the tower clock chimed eight and her reverie was broken by the knowledge that she had only minutes in which to freshen herself.

She splashed some water on her face, recalling with irony how much time she had given to dressing for that disastrous dinner with Joe and how little she had for this vitally important evening with Chad. Shaking her head, she looked into the mirror. She would just have to make do.

Soon her hair was brushed into a glowing cloud and she had added fresh lipstick and a touch of color to her cheeks. Her navy-blue suit, however, caused Katherine to scowl. It was so plain and tailored. Experimenting, she unbuttoned the jacket as far as she dared and, on impulse, pulled fresh violets from a vase and pinned them at the base of the jacket's new neckline. Much better, she decided, and arching her long neck, she applied a few dabs of a favorite scent. Yes, the décolletage made all the difference.

The driver arrived, announcing himself with a series of loud raps at the door. He greeted Katherine with little more than a nod and indicated that she was to follow him. Katherine was relieved by his silence; she was in no mood for idle talk. When they reached the lemon-yellow sports car and the man gestured for her to sit in one of the bucket seats, she hoped with all her might that he would keep his lips as tightly sealed throughout their brief journey.

Soon they were moving swiftly up Wilshire Boulevard, turning right on San Vincente and then whipping smoothly onto Burton Way. Even though the man who sat beside her had barely uttered a word, Katherine still found that butterflies were assailing her stomach. Did Chad want to see her or not? Their phone conversation had been rather confusing, but, she had to admit, she had not helped matters with her own teasing.

They had reached Doheny Drive, on the edge of Beverly Hills. The car wheeled to the right, narrowly missing an elderly couple. The driver coolly ignored their shrill shouts and drove on, continuing his brisk pace across the broad neon strip of Sunset Boulevard and up into a rich, exclusive residential area.

Katherine took a quick breath. The moment of seeing Chad was coming closer, and when the car approached an incredible glass house that cascaded in four glittering levels down a hillside amid fountains, gardens, and trees, Katherine knew that the moment for which she had been waiting was at hand. The driver opened her door with straight-faced formality, but Katherine took no notice. Across a wooden bridge two enormous carved doors were opening, emitting a golden light that warmed the night and silhouetted a tall, strong figure who was striding forward to greet her.

"At last!" Chad exclaimed with pleasure.

Katherine tried to respond and found herself speechless, or at least afraid of what her lips might say as she filled her eyes with Chad. His face was somewhat leaner than before and there were lines of tiredness about his mouth, but his startling good looks were undiminished. Tonight he had dressed as if for a special occasion and his dark raw-silk evening suit made Katherine feel unaccustomedly shy and self-conscious about her own appearance.

"Let me look at you." He drew her into the entry and placed her handbag and briefcase on a table. Very solemnly he gathered her hands into his, just as he had when they were last together, and looked deeply into her eyes. This time, instead of being afraid, Katherine allowed her eyes to answer with eagerness and warmth, yet, for some reason, Chad did not read the message she was trying to give him.

Helplessly, her thoughts awhirl in confusion, Katherine watched as Chad's smile disappeared and was replaced by an expression of harsh displeasure.

"I'm glad to find you looking so well," he said, sounding disappointed. "I must admit, I thought handling Eleanor's and Dee's work, as well as your own, might tire you—at least a bit. But one look and it's clear, you're thriving on all of this, aren't you?"

His voice was filled with accusation, and Katherine nodded her head, not able to understand why. "I've loved it," she said to reassure him, and instantly realized she had somehow said the wrong thing. "But I couldn't keep up this pace all the time."

"It's good to hear that something is too much for you. Otherwise someone might confuse you with the Amazon queen."

His sarcasm stung painfully, and all of the eagerness faded from Katherine's face. What was wrong? Had Chad invited her just to spar with words? If so, it was a game she refused to play.

"Butler's is a wonderful company to work for," she replied stiffly and thought of the irony of defending the company to its president. "I've been both lucky and glad to have a working chance at inheriting Dee's job, and if I am taken on permanently, it will be the biggest thing that has ever happened to me."

"Do you really want to spend your life being another Eleanor?" Chad's voice was strangely pleading.

"I don't see where what I do with my life is of any concern to you." The defiant words were no sooner out of her mouth than Katherine hated herself for being such a fool. But the damage had been done.

Chad had been looking into her face with an intensity that frightened. Suddenly he dropped her hands, almost throwing them at her, and turned away.

"Let's get some champagne."

He walked down the hall, leaving Katherine to decide for herself if she would follow. For a moment she stood alone and miserable, wondering what had happened. Chad had been glad to see her; he had certainly made that obvious. Then what had happened to make him become so cold and disdainful? It would do no good to stand there, she decided. If there was any chance at all of reclaiming the evening from ruin, she had better do her best to please him.

Chad stood waiting in the vast living room. He was holding two glasses of champagne. "Here." He thrust one of the glasses at her. "This is supposed to be a celebration."

Katherine accepted the tall, slender glass gratefully. Watching the bubbles fly magically to the surface, where they exploded to tickle her lips, gave her senses something pleasant to feel in contrast to the stabbing hurt that Chad had dealt her.

Quietly Katherine sipped the pale liquid, allowing it to run down her throat in a thin stream, creating a comforting warm pool somewhere deep inside. All too soon she was ready for another glass and Chad gave it to her.

He was watching her again, his face a cold and arrogant mask. Katherine drank deeply; for the moment it was so much easier to drink champagne than to try to solve Chad's bad temper. When the glass was empty, she lifted her eyes and was going to ask for another, but instead she found the room lurching in circles.

"Steady there!" Chad reached out to prevent her from tottering. "I do believe that our very competent Miss Dunn has drunk her champagne too quickly and needs a little assistance over to a chair."

As he helped her across the room Chad's whole demeanor relaxed and Katherine was glad for her silly wave of dizziness. It had given the evening a second chance. She would do her best not to irritate him again.

After assisting Katherine into a deep armchair, Chad seated himself in the one adjacent. "I shouldn't have refilled your glass," he apologized. "You probably haven't eaten in hours and the stuff was bound to go to your head. Are you feeling better?"

"I'm fine, really. Don't worry." Katherine gave him her warmest smile. "Silly, wasn't I? Drinking it down like lemonade. I promise not to do that again."

"You can collapse in my arms anytime, Katherine." Chad was smiling too. "As a matter of fact it's getting to be a habit I rather like." He gave her an odd, penetrating look and added, "You know there's nothing quite like a damsel in distress to make a man feel needed."

Katherine did not know what kind of answer she was supposed to give. In self-defense she focused on the view through the glass. It was Los Angeles lighting the night with a varied brilliance that challenged the Milky Way.

"I tried to get hold of Joe." Chad broke the silence. "But he was nowhere to be found."

"Jessica Spencer wanted to visit Cielo. I asked Joe to be her guide." Katherine noted another reason to be grateful to Jessica. How hideously awkward it would have been to have Joe here!

"That explains it." Chad laughed. "I'm beginning to think that Joe has every potential of becoming an aging roué."

"You never know. He might find the right woman and get married," Katherine countered, raising an eyebrow knowingly.

"That'll be the day." Chad laughed and was still laughing when the man who had driven Katherine from the office to the house appeared in the doorway and gave Chad a discreet sign.

"Thanks, Jacob. Come along, Miss Dunn, you are about to be treated to the work of an artist." Chad took her arm possessively and guided her into the opulent dining room, where a long ebony table had been set for two.

The scent of roses filled the air and candles competed with the glow from the world beyond the wall of glass.

As soon as Katherine tasted the deliciously buttery stuffed mushrooms, she knew the meaning of Chad's comment. Each succeeding course was a new delight.

"With an appetite like yours no one could accuse you of being in love," Chad said as he watched her finish the last morsel of chocolate mousse pie.

Katherine colored. If only he knew the true state of her emotions!

"Umm, but this is so good! How could anyone not eat every single bite?" she asked, hoping he would not have noticed her hesitation. "Please give your cook my compliments."

"Thank you." Chad bowed his head slightly.

"You're not saying that you did this?" Katherine asked, incredulous.

"Would you believe me if I said I did?"

"No," she answered without hesitation.

"Really? And I thought I had you fooled. You're right. Octavia's gets the credit," he told her, naming one of the city's most famous restaurants. "All I have to do is order on the phone and they deliver. So, you see, no cook. Just you and me and Jacob." Chad nodded to the shadows by the doorway and the enigmatic Jacob stepped forward.

"Fill our glasses, then leave the bottle with me," Chad ordered, gesturing to the wine. "We won't need you again tonight."

Katherine watched as Jacob replenished their wine, placed the bottle close to Chad, and silently slipped off to his own quarters. Now she and Chad were alone—no cook, no Jacob, just the two of them—and outside the black velvet night was studded with stars and city lights, all merging in a dazzling display.

She lifted her glass and held it by the delicate stem,

slowly turning it in her fingers and watching the rich ruby wine glow warmly in the candlelight. After her experience with the champagne Katherine knew that she should be careful, but looking across at Chad's handsome face, she was in no mood for caution. Deliberately she took a sip and allowed it to roll across her tongue. The taste was as warm as the color. She looked again at Chad and her eyes held a bold dare.

"You haven't asked how I could be so certain that you didn't cook our meal." This new boldness felt good; she was enjoying herself.

"No, I guess I haven't." Chad was sitting back in his chair and the candlelight could not reach the shadows of his face.

"Because cooking takes a great deal of creativity, and men just aren't as creative as women." She had said that with a saucy little toss of her head, but when she saw that he continued to sit there, motionless, hidden by the darkness, her nerve began to fail her, and when he leaned forward to reach his glass, all of her bravado disappeared.

"I must disagree, my little Katherine."

She could see the white of his teeth across the table, but the expression in his eyes remained hidden.

"I have a great deal of creative ability." His voice rumbled, low and suggestive. "Let's toast creativity." Chad lifted his wineglass and nodded to Katherine.

Her heart was in her throat as she lifted her glass in response. She wanted desperately to do the right thing, to show him that she really cared.

Chad had moved fully into the arc of candlelight, and while drinking deeply from his glass, he never wavered his gaze from Katherine. His expression seemed to soften as he placed the emptied glass back on the table and reached across the table in search of her hand. Katherine saw the

145

tenderness in his face and her heart leaped with joy as he took her cold fingers into his warm and solid grasp.

"Katherine," he whispered, and the expression in his eyes turned her limp. "I can't stop remembering—"

She wanted him so badly, yet his words made her afraid and her hand stiffened with apprehension. The tenderness in Chad's face evaporated and releasing her hand, he retreated back into his chair.

"You know, China is a fascinating country," he began, as though the last few moments had not occurred, and launched into a detailed account of his most recent visit.

Katherine listened to every word without hearing one. Her thoughts were with other memories: Chad carrying her on that first day when she had twisted her ankle; Cielo, where she had learned the passionate fire of his kisses; Carmel, where she had felt the strength of his arms as they had danced; and, lastly, when he had pulled her from treacherous water and made her his own. She blushed at this favorite of all memories.

When they had finished coffee, Chad announced that he had a surprise, and once again taking Katherine's hand, he led her down the wide stairway to his own room. Katherine was instantly reminded of their day at Cielo and her heart fluttered with hope. Could the magic passion of Cielo and their hidden beach be recaptured?

Chad flicked a switch and the lights revealed an immense room, even larger than the one at Cielo. Here, like everywhere else in the house, the furnishings were starkly modern. Katherine noted that on this, the lowest of the four levels, the glass walls were discreetly hidden from prying eyes by flowering shrubbery, which sent its sweet jasmine perfume in to fill the room.

Chad opened the door to a large dressing room and invited Katherine to follow. Again visions of Cielo fell before her eyes; when they cleared, she saw, hanging against the wall, three large garment bags. On the floor nearby was a magnificent lacquered box inlaid with pearls and precious stones.

"Here it is, Katherine." Chad quickly removed the cases and revealed three jewel-colored silk gowns. "Here is our China Line!"

Katherine gasped. They were beautiful, even hanging lifeless along a wall. The flow of silk from shoulder to hem demonstrated Karen Su's perfection of cut; the colors were so breathtaking that they could not help but win enthusiastic approval.

Chad lifted the first dress and brought it to where Katherine could finger the damask and see clearly the subtle interweaving of the Butler *B* into an overall pattern. "What do you think?"

"I think they're fabulous!" Katherine answered earnestly. Her eyes slid down to the lacquered chest. "Did the jewelry turn out as well?"

"Of course." His dark eyes were flashing with enthusiasm. "I'll show them to you in a minute, but first tell me which of these three you like the best."

Katherine looked at each carefully. It was almost impossible to make a choice. There was a lustrous red caftan, lined in rich turquoise; a green one, even more brilliant then her own silk dress, and beautifully contrasted by its lining of opalescent white; and the third was a purple, more richly royal than any color she had seen before, made even more opulent by its lining of gold.

"Do you really insist that I select just one?"

"That's right." Chad leaned back against the wall, watching her, his arms crossing his broad chest.

Katherine reexamined each gown and sighed in dismay. She could only hope that Butler's customers found The China Line as irresistible as she did.

."All right, if I have to make a choice, it will be the purple."

"Good." Chad nodded approval. "I agree. That's the best color for you."

Katherine turned her wide green eyes upon him. What was this all about?

"All of the time I was in China, working with thousands of these, preparing them for shipping, I kept wondering what one would look like on a beautiful woman, and you, my dear, are going to show me." He was eyeing her with that unreadable expression again, and Katherine was caught in the compelling pull of his magnetic charm.

"You know you have to pay for your supper in some way." He had picked up the lacquered box and was opening it.

"I thought I was your guest," Katherine said bravely, trying to fight against the implications of his comment.

A crooked smile, faintly tainted with wickedness, twisted at Chad's lips. "Didn't anyone ever tell you that nothing is for free?"

Katherine became silent. Was it a joke? Was all he really wanted a modeling of the gowns? Or did she dare to hope that the question that simmered so provocatively in his eyes had a meaning that was quite different? A shiver of excitement raced down her spine.

The box Chad had opened nearly overflowed with a shimmering bonanza of pearls and jade. With the practiced eye of a connoisseur he picked through the treasure trove, at last deciding upon a wide choker of tiny pearls from which hung a luminous pink jade intricately and beautifully cut into the famous Butler *B*. To this he added a rope of larger pearls.

"These ought to be right." He handed the jewelry to Katherine, another crooked smile revealing the edges of his strong, white teeth.

"I'd offer to stay and help you put them on, but I'm sure you'd prefer I went upstairs to wait." Chad turned to leave and Katherine felt almost faint with relief, but he was not finished with her yet.

"Just don't keep me waiting too long," he drawled, giving the words a deliberate ambiguity.

Alone Katherine began to undress, placing her navy suit carefully on an extra hanger. Carmel and the events that had occurred there were more alive in her mind than ever before. For weeks she had been dreaming of his touch. Could it be that tonight she would thrill to it once again?

Katherine's senses could not forget the gentleness of Chad's first kisses; nor could they forget the ruthless, unyielding demand of the later ones. Would these moods be relived tonight? The sensible side of her nature said go home now, while you are still safe. But now there was another side to Katherine, a side that Chad had discovered and awakened, and this part of her tingled with excitement and longing.

A jolting thought struck her: her daydreams could be wrong. Maybe Chad thought of this strictly as business and she had taught him the lesson all too well. And what about Carole Seeley? What was their relationship? A bitter taste invaded her mouth as she recalled that night in Carmel and how easily Carole had captivated both Chad and Joe. How could someone like herself hope to compete with Carole Seeley, a woman so daring that beneath the smooth fall of her dress she had been naked?

Suddenly Katherine made a decision. If that was the way Chad liked his women, she could do it too.

Deliberately she shed every bit of clothing she had worn, leaving even her shoes behind. But before slipping into the caftan she turned to a wall mirror and studied her own white body, just as she had done at Cielo. She remembered her thoughts and doubts then. They were no less now. Did she know what she was doing? Katherine lowered her eyes and turned away.

When she stepped, barefooted, onto the tantalizing softness of the living room carpet, she found the atmosphere quite changed. There was only one light to guide her and the rest of the room fell into shadow.

Katherine moved in trembling steps to where the one beacon promised safety. She searched the darkness for Chad and finally found him outlined, a massive shadow, against the twinkling glimmer that spread beyond the glass. She waited for him to speak, but everywhere there was silence, and the only sound to reach her ears was her own pulse throbbing within her head.

Tension magnified and continued to build as Katherine stood hopelessly waiting, like a sacrificial lamb awaits the lion.

The shadow moved. Chad stepped within the arc of light. He stopped and sipped thoughtfully from a brandy snifter.

"Turn," he commanded, gesturing a circle with his free hand.

Katherine obeyed, fighting to retain her poise. He had told her to model The China Line, now that was what she must do. Carefully, but with the smooth flow of a seasoned professional, Katherine moved in sweeping circles. She lifted an arm to show the tapered cut of the sleeve and, with the twist of her head and touch of her fingers, focused attention on the pearls and jade that graced her neck.

"Stop. Now!" Chad ordered. "Don't move even a hair." His voice sounded strange and husky, not like him at all. Katherine wondered how much he had been drinking.

"I want to see you this way and remember. The light, the way it falls upon your hair and outlines your whole being . . . the gorgeous bones of your face . . . the promise

150

of your—" He paused and she could feel his gaze burning through the silk.

Her heart skipped a beat and in that moment he was before her. The fire in his eyes was sweeping over her, consuming what little courage remained and leaving her weak-kneed and afraid.

This was not the Chad of the gentle kisses. This was the Chad whose blood coursed like a red-hot river, driving him to demand all that she could ever give.

He seemed to sense her fear and stepped back, lifting the glass one more time, but the moment did not last.

Katherine searched his face for an expression, a small sign of assurance. There was none. Yet, as he neared, she found her fear dissolved and turned into yearning. His hand reached out and touched her chin, tilting it upward. Katherine did not want to close her eyes. She wanted to watch Chad's lips, warm and sensual, as they came closer, descending upon her own in a kiss so filled with gentle desire that she would remember it forever.

"Katherine, Katherine." He repeated her name again and again, moving his lips up over her cheek and into her hair. "I want you more than anything."

His hand was on her shoulder and gliding powerfully downward, pulling her closer into his embrace. Shivers of delight followed the pressure of his fingers as his hand dipped dangerously over her hip. Katherine threw aside any pretense of resistance and in glorious abandon lifted her face in search of his lips. They were there, eager and waiting, and when they came together, a fire burst within her, filling every vein with wild desire.

Chad's needs were even greater than her own, and when he lifted her into his arms, she knew exactly where he was taking her. Arching her back, she pulled herself even closer to him, responding to his insistent kisses with demands all her own.

At the base of the stairs Chad kicked open the door to his room and carried Katherine to the bed. Gently he lay her down and stood over her.

Katherine was lost in her own blur of happiness. Never had she felt more like a woman, and she hoped that she looked as sensuous as she felt. Her red hair was fanned out upon the dark coverlet, and the marvelous silk of the caftan caressed her skin, a seductive prelude to the touch of Chad's hands.

She reached up to him, longing to feel him in her embrace. He came down to her, his eyes burning into hers. She felt her fingers curl through his hair and lock behind his neck. She drew him closer, lifting her lips to meet his. When they touched, Katherine closed her eyes and surrendered completely.

Deftly Chad undressed her, slipping the silk gown down from her shoulders and baring her white breasts.

"You are even more beautiful this time," he murmured as he began to slowly caress her soft flesh with his lips, lingering at the crowns of each breast and tantalizing them with the feverish stroking of his tongue.

Katherine whimpered and writhed beneath him, unable to respond so long as he kept her arms pinned to her sides.

"All right," he whispered. "Don't be so impatient. You'll soon have your turn."

In moments they were intertwined, and Katherine was allowed to revel in the feel of Chad's strong body beneath her fingertips.

"You witch! You drive me mad," he hissed and brought his mouth down upon hers in a kiss so fierce that it brought tears of pain and a faint taste of blood.

"Chad, please!"

"Yes, Chad pleases!" he hissed again and with sure strokes lifted Katherine to a state of passion he had not shown her before. Yet even as she approached a crest,

Katherine could not completely free herself of a gnawing uncertainty. Why was Chad being so brutal?

"Damn!" he cursed and pulled himself from her. The phone was ringing relentlessly. "Don't move! I'll be right back."

Katherine waited impatiently, watching him through eyes blurred with love. How magnificent he was—his broad shoulders, narrow hips, and long, powerful legs. She wanted him to hurry back to her no matter her vague misgivings, until his words dispelled all desire.

"I didn't know you were coming," Chad spoke into the phone and to Katherine's chagrin his voice was filled with pleasant surprise. After some time he spoke again, saying, "Of course I will. When do you want me?" Then, finally, he added, "I'll be right there."

He hung up the phone, looking thoughtful. It was several seconds before he seemed to remember that she was even there.

"Oh!" he said abruptly. "Sorry, but you had better get dressed." He reached for the phone again. "I'll have Jacob drive you back. I have to change my plans."

CHAPTER NINE

Down they plunged. Down into the night. As far as Katherine was concerned, Jacob could not drive fast enough.

She was making her ignominious return to the city. Away from the glittering palace on the hill, where as a woman, as a lover, she had been sampled, as a new wine might be tasted, and found wanting. Spat out and rejected, she was being returned to the real world, where people rose and worked each day for their bread at night.

Well, she thought with bitter cynicism, for a discarded and tainted woman she was certainly being delivered back into obscurity in grandiose style.

The Butlers had managed to produce yet one more car. This one was a silver limousine equipped with all of the luxurious amenities so much a part of super-rich life, and Katherine resented every one of them. There was the lacquered wood interior, Moroccan leather upholstery, telephone, television—who knew where the bar was hidden—and, most evocative of all, a panel of handsomely etched glass separating the driver from the parvenus who languished uselessly in the rear. All of these her angry eyes surveyed and analyzed. As a member of the "have-nots," she found it easy to hate the "haves."

Katherine emitted a mirthless chuckle. The glass panel, what a perfect cutoff it made for Jacob—and of course he had it closed.

Sullenly she stared out into the city, which glided silently by their speeding car. He was traveling fast, she acknowledged as Jacob swerved into another, faster lane and Katherine was shifted into a padded armrest. Their trip to her apartment would take less than the twenty minutes of their first excursion.

Katherine wondered, a wry twist turning her lips, why Jacob should be in such a hurry. Was he simply anxious to rid her from their lives, or was it something else? Perhaps Chad wanted his driver back quickly for his own purposes. That mysterious phone conversation had made one thing clear: Someone was summoning him and he was being more than obliging.

She buried her face in her hands at the memory of the horrid chill in his last words. And now she felt almost nauseated with self-disgust, because, despite the awful way in which Chad had abused her, she still loved him. There was no denying it. The door to her emotions had been opened and the demons of her heart were free. She would be forever hounded by her own weakness and the terrible reality that where Chad Butler was concerned she would always be vulnerable.

Looking beyond the tinted window, Katherine saw the tapering silhouette of Butler's loom out of the darkness. Begrudgingly she admired the elegant architectural proportions, then watched, with startled eyes, as a blaze of lights illuminated the seventh-floor roof—the level on which the heliport was located.

Suddenly Chad's phone conversation began to echo in her head. "When do you want me?" he had asked. The person to whom he had been speaking must have been eager, because he had immediately promised to be "right there." Fear twisted at her stomach as she watched the lighted rooftop recede into the distance, and thoughts of Cielo, so intimately secluded beneath the velvet sky, filled her mind with tormenting images. One thing she felt was certain: Chad's companion would be a woman.

The car turned off of Wilshire and Katherine could see that they were only blocks from her apartment. A traffic signal at the corner was turning red, and when Jacob brought them to a stop, she pushed the rear door open and ran sobbing into the dark street.

Katherine found the night a horror and the morning even worse. There was no awakening fresh and rested as she had planned, because there was no sleep. Instead she spent the long hours between midnight and the first gray light of dawn tossing restlessly, her entire being trapped in seething conflict. Peace was unattainable while the wholeness of her nature was split asunder.

Katherine's body still tingled with the unfulfilled passion Chad had awakened from slumbering to this savage state of torment. Yet her conscience clashed violently against such shameless desires.

The clock's dial approached five thirty, and Katherine, grateful that the morning had finally come, arose to face the most important day of her career.

There it was, she thought, that same question once again. Which was more important in her life: her career or Chad Butler? Now that it was too late to have any meaning, the answer had become painfully clear.

Absently Katherine pulled her tan slacks and madras jacket from the closet. Dee had been right after all, she thought as she buttoned her white crepe blouse with extra determination. This was no time to cry, as her aching

156

heart demanded. Tears could come later. Hurriedly she finished dressing and readied herself for the long day ahead.

Butler's, before hours, was entered by means of a special electronic card-key. Katherine used it and rode directly to the seventh floor.

The heliport was teeming with activity. All kinds of materials, equipment, and people were being readied for departure. Katherine extracted her checklist and moved between groups of technicians, cameramen, fitters, hair-stylists, and the makeup team. She wondered if the public could ever guess what planning and effort went into pro-ducing the ads that looked desirably glamorous but oh so casual and easy to emulate when viewed on television or in magazines and newspapers.

Finishing her tour, Katherine saw that her list checked out almost perfectly. All that were missing were the three principals: Chad, Joe, and their model, Jessica Spencer. She was not concerned about Joe and Jessica. They were both reliable. So, too, was Chad, she thought resolutely. He could be relied upon to cut out her heart and serve it for breakfast.

Katherine shook her head fiercely. This attitude of self-pity would not do. She must swallow back her heartbreak and pretend, for all the world to see, that Katherine Dunn was the successful, efficient professional she had sought to be.

It was with this resolve that Katherine boarded the first of the large transport helicopters, rented for the day, and flew to Casa del Cielo. She had made the flight several times during the past few weeks in preparation for this day, but each time, for her, was like the first flight to Cielo and that first wonderful day alone with Chad when they had come so close—No! Those thoughts could not be dwelt upon any longer. She sighed, frowning with self-reproach, and determinedly opened her briefcase to review, once again, the schedule for the day. All of the photography was to be shot in the open and it was a relief to see that the weather was bright, warm, and cloudless.

The helicopter began its descent and Katherine looked down at Cielo awakening in the early morning sun with beads of evaporating dew bejeweling the red tiles of its roof. Suddenly her heart leaped within her breast. The red helicopter was nowhere to be seen. Nor was there any other sign of life. Maybe she had been wrong about Chad's coming here, a small voice whispered eagerly in her head. Then a larger, more rational voice asked what that would mean. Only that Chad had gone somewhere else.

Upon landing, the crew unloaded reflectors, cameras, and additional lighting onto a flatbed truck, which would haul the equipment to the photo site. Katherine left them to their work. It was just eight o'clock; three full hours remained before photography would start. There was plenty of time for her to make a cup of coffee.

She unlocked the door, using the key Chad had loaned her. Inside, the air was old and stale, another good sign. Katherine smiled involuntarily as she strolled toward the kitchen and allowed her eyes to rove through each room, checking to make sure that all was in order. At last her gaze moved out the glass walls and into the patio where the tropical garden beckoned invitingly, and where a terrible shock awaited.

Katherine stopped, incredulous. Perhaps, she thought, if she were to pinch herself, she would awaken and leave this nightmare behind. The nightmare of Carole Seeley draped languidly atop a garden chaise, her tanned body covered only by a towel.

Their eyes met. Katherine realized, frowning with distaste, that Carole had probably been watching her every move. Carole's provocative mouth was curved in a purely feline smile.

"Come on out. The weather's fine," she called.

Katherine searched to find an open door and went out to meet her nemesis.

"My, my." Carole chuckled mockingly. "You don't seem glad to see me. And here I've been waiting ages for you to come." She paused to create an exaggerated pouting expression.

"What time is it?" she asked and, quick as a panther's paw, flicked Katherine with her claws by adding sweetly, "Chad said you would be early."

No matter the cost in hurt, Katherine would not be baited. Instead she raked her foe with hard eyes. There seemed to be no purpose in hiding her aversion.

"What are you doing here?"

"Why, Katherine darling, haven't you been told? I'm to be your model."

"Where's Jessica?" Katherine demanded, a growing panic gnawing at her smooth facade.

"Poor Jessica, she's been hurt." Carole watched Katherine, her eyes mere slits against the sun. "You should never have sent her up here, Katherine. You know our little Jessica is too tender a plant for this terrain. Even that nice Joe couldn't save her from falling and breaking her arm."

Carole lifted a slim hand to shade her eyes. "Lucky, isn't it, that I was so conveniently nearby—just down the road on a Palm Springs assignment. Anyway," she sighed, "I'm sure you're dying to know, my answering service gave me the message and I flew into town as fast as I could arrange it. After all, dear Katherine, you know what a loyal friend I am. And, you should know by now, I never refuse Chad when he needs me."

The cunning triumph in her voice was almost more than

Katherine could take. As if to emphasize her advantage, Carole raised herself to a seated position, allowing her towel to drop and reveal her lush golden body. Katherine gasped audibly, much to her tormentor's delight, and Carole curled her red lips to show her famous smile.

"Last night," she hissed softly, "this morning; and, I plan, forever, Chad needs *me.*"

All the while she spoke, Carole never moved her eyes from Katherine's face, and as she saw the expression of horror widen, she began to laugh, a deep, almost primitive laugh that was both insolent and without shame.

Katherine clasped her hands to her ears and whirled to seek escape.

"You are a stupid fool," Carole called after her in a taunting jeer. "Did you really think that Chad Butler could ever want you?"

Stumbling in a blind and mindless flight, Katherine reached the main doors and, after stepping through, slammed them hard upon Carole's vile laughter and her own wistful dreams. She took refuge in the recesses of the shaded porch, wanting to regain her calm before having to rejoin the crowd preparing for the shooting. While she nursed the throbbing ache echoing in her head, a familiar red helicopter dropped out of the sky and the throb in her temple picked up its beat.

Joe Parkman was the first to climb out. He looked both agitated and concerned. Chad soon followed: lean, massive, devastatingly handsome in a dark gray suit whose expensive cut only served to emphasize a pair of extremely broad shoulders. The two men mingled casually with the crews loading the trucks, and then, spying Katherine, they moved toward the shade of the porch.

"Did you hear about Jessica?" Joe called to her anxiously. "Poor girl, it's a bad break. But her only concern is that she's let you down, Katherine." He turned to Chad and asked a question, which he had obviously already answered in his own mind. "Can you imagine anyone more sweet and loyal and loving than Jessica?"

Katherine remained silent, watching Chad to see if he appeared different after the activities he must have experienced during the night. His eyes were still smoldering and he was equally solemn as he looked at her.

"Wasn't it fortunate that Carole was so available?" he asked sardonically, holding Katherine in his melting gaze.

Katherine averted her eyes to the wooden planking of the porch. She did not want to answer, but Chad was not to be denied. Audaciously he reached for her and lifted her chin with brash familiarity.

"As a good businesswoman you can't deny that this was a stroke of luck, can you, Katherine Dunn?"

She wrenched free of his touch. If there had been the slightest suggestion of the compassion and tenderness he had shown he possessed, Katherine would have thrown away all pride and told him everything. Instead his facial mien was cold, his bearing thoroughly arrogant. All that was left to her was a brave show of professionalism.

"Yes, yes. You're quite right," she agreed, nearly choking on her words but managing to sound entirely credible. "In fact—not meaning to offend you, Joe—but having Carole will bring The China Line even more attention than if we had used Jessica."

She turned back to Chad with a determined nonchalance. "Where are the caftans and the jewelry?" she asked, pretending she had never seen them before. "You said that you would bring them."

"Don't worry, they're here—in my bedroom." All warmth had left his eyes and his mouth was hard and dour until it twisted nastily when he added, "You remember where my bedroom is."

Katherine wanted to slap him. His tone was so offen-

161

sive. How dare he hint of their intimacy with Joe present! Whatever his feelings were for her, she would not permit him to tarnish her memories—not when they were all she had left.

"Excuse me, gentlemen." She eyed them coldly. "I must get back to work and find the fitters. Those caftans will need pressing before Carole puts them on."

Katherine moved away from the shaded porch, forcing herself to walk in smooth and even steps, and headed for the transport copter that had just arrived. Luckily the fitters were among the first to disembark and she had just finished talking with them when an unexpected voice startled her.

"Adam, this place is so remote. Imagine having to fly in! Why doesn't Chad build some roads?"

Eleanor Graham climbed awkwardly down to the ground. Behind her stepped Adam Butler, his urbane good looks accentuated by Eleanor's rumpled, ill-fitting suit and untamed hair. Katherine noted the look of strain about Adam's eyes and the tenseness of his mouth.

Adam had seen her. He smiled without showing much enthusiasm and waved rather perfunctorily. It was Eleanor who greeted her with a wide smile of apparent delight.

"Katherine! How good it is to see you!" she hailed, advancing from the propeller's shadow, her arms open in anticipation. "My, you have done well," she proclaimed in a loud voice as she reached Katherine and embraced her in an unwanted hug. "I can see you haven't missed me a bit, eh?" Eleanor laughed heartily and backed away to look up at Katherine with a smile that might have been convincing if Katherine had not caught the chilling glint in the overly bright eyes.

"What a wonderful surprise," Katherine managed as a feeble response while edging herself to a safer distance.

Adam placed his hand upon her shoulder as if he

162

thought she might run. "Come now, Katherine," he chided in a tired voice. "You didn't really think that even a presidential conference could keep us from such an important event. Why, this is a historic day for Butler's."

"It certainly is," Eleanor agreed, her peculiarly sinister smile falling once again upon Katherine. "This is a day that none of us will ever forget."

"Where is Chad?" Adam changed the subject abruptly as he gently guided Eleanor away from Katherine.

"He's up at the—"

"You can see Chad any time." Eleanor interrupted. "It's this China Line I'm interested in. Where are you keeping the gowns, Katherine?"

"Oh, they're all in Chad's room," Katherine answered absently, still staring at the woman. What had happened? Eleanor had never asked about The China Line before. What was behind this sudden interest? Katherine turned puzzled eyes to Adam, but he, too, was watching Eleanor.

Eleanor had started to walk away.

"Where are you going?" Adam asked.

"To the house," she called over her shoulder. "I'm tired. Think I'll take a nap."

Katherine wanted to ask Adam what was going on, but he had already started after Eleanor. She watched them disappear into the shade of the porch, a frown creasing her brow. She would just have to ask Adam later; for now there were too many other things that needed doing. Among these chores was overseeing the transport of Carole Seeley's portable dressing room, and it was some time before she could return to the house.

When she did return, it was to find Carole holding court. The hair stylists and makeup men were dancing attendance, while Joe and Adam watched admiringly. But it was to Chad that Carole was playing.

Just one quick look was enough for Katherine. The very

way that Chad was standing, his tall hard frame leaning against a wall and his dark eyes resting solely on Carole, was more than enough proof of his interest in her brazen sensuality.

Katherine swallowed hard. Carefully she avoided attracting attention and slipped around to the study, where she found the fitters engaged in playing cards. The China gowns, they told her, had long since been pressed and were waiting for her in Mr. Butler's dressing room.

Katherine approached the closed door of Chad's bedroom with uneasiness. Not only was she going to face those memories of that other, very special day, but she fully expected to find Eleanor sleeping. Katherine had been keeping an eye out for her but so far Eleanor was nowhere to be seen. But as she opened the door she saw that the room was empty.

Chad's bedroom was unchanged. The same wolf skin fell upon the bed, and the same wall of mirrors mocked her failure, because now there was a new presence: the heady, possessive, hovering fragrance of Carole Seeley. Katherine had noted it earlier. The aroma lingered everywhere in the home that was now quite obviously Carole's domain.

She bit her lip and turned her attention to the dressing room. The three caftans were waiting, just as the fitters had said, but there was something ghastly in the way the silk fell from the hangers. Fearful of what she might find, Katherine reached out to the shimmering royal purple she had worn so recently. Her eyes grew wide with horror. The dress had been slashed! Not in just one tentative cut either, but in dozens of long rents leading from the hem up over the breast and involving the sleeves too. One sweeping look told her that whoever was vicious enough to vandalize the purple had dealt similar damage to the red and the green gowns.

Katherine swayed from the shock as the jewel-colored ribbons drifted through her fingers. Who? Why? Her head was dizzy with questions and the largest, most demanding question of all was: What to do now? Should they admit a dreadfully costly defeat, or should they try to find a solution? And what could that solution be? Katherine was attempting to sort out the alternatives when Carole came into the dressing room and stood behind her.

"I thought it was time to— Well, well, well, what happened here?" the taunting voice asked as she reached to check the extent of the mutilation. She smiled wickedly, her pink tongue darting between fine white teeth. "I do believe I'm going to be paid for doing what I like best: playing around with Chad Butler." Her eyes flicked over Katherine like a whip. "You really are a fool, Katherine, a silly, bumbling, ineffectual fool. These dresses are ruined and so are you."

Carole strolled leisurely to the door and opened it. "Chad," she called, her voice suddenly filled with pretended horror. "Come quickly! Something awful has happened."

They were all there within seconds: Chad, Adam, Joe. Even the fitters crowded in at the door and finally, arriving just after the others, came Eleanor. While everyone else stared at the damage, Eleanor's eyes darted nervously from face to face.

"Who could have come in here?" she demanded of Katherine. "Didn't you think to assign someone to watch over our merchandise when it isn't being used?"

"Did they get the jewelry too?" Joe asked in a tight voice.

"No. I have not let that box out of my sight." It was Chad's voice and his tone was as hard as steel.

Katherine turned to look at him. Was he accusing her of carelessness as Eleanor already had done? She wanted to answer him, but there was no time to consider the implications of his attitude. From the moment she had recognized the extent of the damage, Katherine had been concentrating upon a single idea. It was a wild one and there was a good chance that either Chad or Adam would vote it down, but it was their only hope of staying on schedule and salvaging the day.

Gently Katherine lifted a handful of the red caftan with its brilliant turquoise lining. The silk had been cut into ribbons, but they were beautiful ribbons and perhaps they could still be used.

Of course it would be necessary to do more photography when the full shipment arrived, but that would not be for several weeks. Meanwhile, by using these and making only minor changes, they could launch the promotion and at the very least establish the theme. It was worth a gamble, and the thought of helping Chad gave her the courage to speak.

"Listen," she told them quietly. "I have an idea." Her eyes searched the room for Chad, but he had disappeared. Katherine's voice cracked with doubt but she went on. "I'm sure it can work."

When she finished her explanation, she waited for a reaction, and Adam's was quick.

"It's worth trying," he agreed. "Too much time and expense have already gone into this day without at least making this effort. I know Chad will agree when I find him. But in the meantime I'll send back one of the men to collect all of those things you need."

Katherine breathed a deep sigh of relief and looked up at Adam with appreciation for his faith in her, then she quickly compiled a list and, after handing it over to one of the pilots, called the fitters together and sketched out on paper exactly what she wanted them to do. The three women were eager to follow Katherine's direction, and as soon as she could be sure that her plan was going to work, Katherine went in search of Carole. The time had come for them to leave for the location site, but she found Carole not the least bit cooperative.

"I'm not going off to that dusty spot to waste my time on your stupid ideas," she declared, almost spitting the words in her anger at the suggestion. But this time it was Katherine who held the trump card.

"It doesn't much matter if you want to go or not, Carole," Katherine said smoothly as she took a firm hold of one slim arm. "You're doing it anyway."

Carole started to pull away and Katherine squeezed her arm harder. "Just remember this: If you don't do your best stuff, your agency is going to hear about it, and that, dear Carole, could put you out on your ear."

Katherine was surprised at her own ferocity. She had never come close to threatening anyone before in her life. But, she consoled herself, this was no threat. It was a very sincere promise. Determinedly she guided a somewhat chastened Carole out of the house and toward a waiting van, one of the many that were acting as shuttles between the heliport and the photography location.

As they stepped away from the shaded porch Katherine saw Joe coming toward them.

"Where's Chad?" she asked anxiously.

"He's been checking up on what happened to those dresses."

"Find him quickly and tell him we need that jewel box up at the location fast!"

Joe turned and loped off to find Chad while Katherine and Carole climbed into the van to join the fitters, makeup team, and hair stylists for the bumpy ride to the valley Chad had selected as the photographic location.

Katherine had brought the gowns with them, and while they waited for the accessories to arrive from Butler's, she

167

explained to Carole the changes that had been made. The threat to report her to the agency appeared to have worked because with the exception of a nasty gleam in her eyes Carole was docile and obliging.

When the messenger arrived, he brought everything Katherine had requested: bright-colored body stockings, tasseled tie belts, and a new line of excitingly exotic high-heeled sandals. Feverish activity filled the dressing area with Katherine rattling off directions to both the fitters and to Carole. When Chad came, bearing the lacquered jewel box, Carole was nearly ready to go before the cameras.

"What do you think?" Katherine asked nervously, searching his face for reaction.

Chad's eyes traveled leisurely over Carole's supple body, and Katherine could not tell whether it was the clothes she wore or the body beneath that was holding his attention.

No denying it, Katherine thought with tired resignation, Carole was beauty incarnate standing posed for Chad's admiring inspection, her lips shining with invitation. But it was the spectacular array of vivid color that Carole wore that held Katherine's attention. A blue-violet second skin covered Carole from shoulder to toe and over it fell the emerald caftan, its shimmering ribbons of green and opalescent white fluttering gracefully about her slim legs.

"It's certainly a change from the original," Chad finally answered, his voice flat and noncommittal. "Here's the jewelry. At least they're still the way Karen Su designed them."

His callous words hurt Katherine like a stinging slap. She took the box from his hands without looking at him and carried it over to the dressing table. When she felt controlled enough to speak to him, she found the doorway empty.

During the shooting Katherine and Joe were everywhere at once: checking each detail, allowing no mistakes.

Periodically Katherine searched the crowd, looking for Chad's face, and each time she found him his expression held only skepticism, even though with everyone's cooperation the photo session went almost as originally planned.

At the end, however, even Katherine could feel the dark mood that had fallen and only Carole Seeley seemed capable of smiling.

At last the dreadful day was over, and Katherine was supervising the packing up of merchandise when Chad arrived. She did not see him enter and only realized his presence when the magic of his nearness caused her blood to throb within her veins. Holding out the jewel box, she found his hands overtaking hers and lifting the box from her trembling fingers, his flesh brushing tantalizingly against hers.

"Katherine." His voice, rough and husky, was calling her name, and with great reluctance she slid her gaze up to his face. His emotions were hidden again in that deep, unreadable expression that never failed to rouse both her desires and her fears.

"I want you to know how grateful Dad and I are for everything you've done." He paused and looked down, a frown creasing his brow. "No matter what happens, we'll still feel that way."

He seemed on the verge of saying more when Carole emerged from behind the changing screen.

"Chad darling, wasn't I marvelous?" She flicked wide eyes at Katherine. "Considering what little I had to work with, everyone is saying my modeling was superb." She had already entwined her arm through Chad's and was pulling her body as near to his as was possible.

Katherine turned away, embarrassed at this brazen display, and continued her packing until Chad's voice interrupted her.

"Excuse us, Katherine, but would you mind? Carole and I need to speak privately."

It was as if an electric current had cut clean through her body, jolting her with one sharp excruciating pain and then leaving her limp and totally numb. Wordlessly Katherine picked up her own few things and the garment bag she had finished packing. The distance between the dressing table and the door was the most dreadful she had ever endured.

Outside, a late autumn sunset was falling, but Katherine's glazed eyes were unappreciative of the red ball sun dropping behind the hilltops. All that she saw was a van moving past, its big wheels squirting gravel and dirt behind. She hailed it to a stop and climbed aboard, grateful that no one she knew was present.

The van jolted forward and Katherine looked out through the dust and watched, her senses deadened, as the dressing room disappeared into the gathering dark along with her dreams.

CHAPTER TEN

"Can I do something to help, Miss Dunn?" a friendly voice spoke out of the darkened doorway.

"Thanks, Arthur." Katherine managed a wan smile. "You can't know how tired I am."

The night watchman lifted the heavy garment bag from her weary arms and led her from the hubbub of the seventh-floor heliport into the hushed quiet of after-hours Butler's. It was a welcome relief. Katherine had fought a case of exhausted nerves all the way back from Cielo. Her one desire now was for privacy.

"Do you want this in your office?" Arthur asked cheerfully, indicating the bag.

Katherine nodded apathetically as they entered the elevator. She leaned her head back, resting it against the teak wood interior, and closed her eyes for the entire descent. The door opened and they stepped out into the great foyer. A wave of dizziness swept over her. It was amazing, she thought, how an empty store could be filled with ghosts.

"How'd it go today?" The watchman's eyes were wide and curious.

They were passing the floor display where Katherine had taken her three fateful steps. If only she could turn that wall clock back and try it all over again. She laughed beneath her breath. As if doing it over would make any difference.

"Rumors were flying when I came on duty." Arthur gave her a sideways glance laced with reproach.

Katherine was too locked into her own reverie to answer. Memories were bittersweet, she thought, but still they should be savored, especially when they were the only solace that remained.

Arthur sighed a reluctant surrender to Katherine's complete lack of response and sauntered on down the aisle, the same aisle over which Chad had carried her. So much had happened in the intervening weeks and yet Katherine could still close her eyes and feel the strength of Chad's arms and hear the pounding beat of his heart.

They had reached Eleanor's office, and the brightness of the lights made Katherine blink defensively. Tonight the all-white room appeared even more frigid and repressive than before.

"It was awfully nice of you to carry that for me," Katherine said, gesturing to where the bag should be hung and offering Arthur another weak smile.

Arthur took it as encouragement. "Everyone's talking and wondering, Miss Dunn." He was looking at her hopefully. "Are the things Mr. Butler brought back from China really as good as he says?"

Katherine averted his eyes. "Of course they are," she answered, edging her words with an obvious frost.

The nightwatchman was not easily discouraged. "Well, you see, Miss Dunn," he persisted, "there's a lot of talk about things going bad."

She turned from him abruptly and walked to the desk she had been using.

"It's been a long day, Arthur, I—" She had started to say that she was too tired to talk, but the boldly written note attached to her day-book caught her attention and held it fast. The note had been placed in such a way that she could see it the moment she reached the desk, and Katherine did not need the initials to know from whom it came.

YOU'RE FIRED.
E.G.

Just two short words and they said it all. How Eleanor must have enjoyed writing it.

Katherine stood staring down at the note, a thousand fragmented thoughts whirring through her mind. All that had happened, for it to end like this. A mirthless laugh slid out of her throat, and she might well have lost control and become hysterical had Arthur not appeared at her shoulder. His curiosity could not be denied nor his almost morbid excitement.

"Oh, my, miss! What are you going to do?"

"I don't know." She shrugged and allowed her shoulders to sag with fatigue. "Go home, I guess." Back to that miserable little town she had left with such high blown dreams, because now the dreams were over and there was nothing left but glaring and ugly reality.

Arthur's eyes bulged nervously. "If there's nothing more you want, Miss Dunn . . ."

Katherine raised a hand to wave him off. "Go," she said. "Go on—and thank you." She was glad to see him back out of the door. Hurrying off to call someone and tell them the latest, she thought unpleasantly.

For a few minutes Katherine allowed herself the luxury

173

of simply sitting, her face buried in her hands. Any other time and tears would be falling freely, but lack of sleep and the effect of the recent grueling events had mercifully numbed her feelings. She found herself able to coolly review the telltale incidents that had run through the day: Adam Butler's hesitant greeting, Eleanor's aura of triumph. They had known when she first saw them that this note was waiting on her desk. Katherine squeezed her eyes shut and breathed deeply, fighting to maintain her calm against the dreadful hurt that threatened when recalling Chad's words. He had not even dared look her in the eye as he had said them: "No matter what happens. . . ." He, too, had known!

She jammed the note into her purse, a saving rage lifting her from lethargy. She would waste no more time in this place! Swiftly she gathered the few signs of her presence and walked out, angrily determined to give no backward glance to the seat of her dead ambitions.

The bus ride home dissipated the strengthening anger and left her aware only of how totally alone she was. The driver, her fellow passengers, they were strangers. It was always this way, only tonight it served to reinforce her feeling of helplessness and empty defeat.

Slowly the emotions that had so mercifully been numbed came back to life, and as Katherine walked, unseeing, down her street the tears, which she had held bravely back, emerged victorious to flood her eyes and fall in riverlets upon her cheeks. A small car came speeding by. Its headlights illuminated Katherine's vulnerability, but for the first time in her life she did not care, and she was too blinded by her tears to see the driver.

The apartment house loomed large and unfriendly, its long narrow hallway dimly lit. Tonight it seemed more lonely than before as Katherine walked slowly to her door at the far end. Her key slid easily into the lock. She turned

174

it, longing only for a hot bath and bed. She turned it again and cried out with frustration. The lock was jammed. It happened regularly, but this time it was the last straw and Katherine fell against the offending door, sobbing great gusts of tears.

Then, with the shocking menace of the unexpected, Katherine felt a hand grab her shoulder, clutch it in a grip of steel, and now a new terror was added to her hysteria. She opened her mouth to scream and a second powerful hand clamped it rudely shut. Someone was urging her to be quiet, but like a wild thing she fought against the hopeless strength of her assailant, scratching and clawing at a face she could not see. She felt her nails cut into flesh and heard a muttered curse of pain. Then her tormentor's words came to her ears clearly and through the haze of her fear and despondency she recognized the voice.

"Katherine!" Chad was shaking her. "Stop it!"

Her teeth rattled in her head and her whole being was set quivering by Chad's continued shaking.

"No more," she pleaded. "You're hurting me."

"Ha! You little vixen, as if you can't do your own share of hurting."

Katherine turned to face him and saw that he was nursing a cheek with his handkerchief. Even so, blood had dripped onto his snowy shirt collar.

"Oh!" she gasped, putting her hand to her mouth. "I didn't mean to—"

"Didn't you?" Chad's voice was cold and angry. He searched her face as if looking for an answer in the soft turn of her mouth. "Good God, girl! What got into you? All I did was put my hand on your shoulder and suddenly I find myself fighting a wildcat."

Down the hall a door opened, sending a slice of light across the corridor. An old woman stepped out and riveted them with her beady look of disapproval. "I'm report-

175

ing this to the manager in the morning," she called to Katherine in a high, thin voice. "We've never had your sort here before."

Chad swung to face the old woman, his powerful shoulders tensed with anger. She paled and like a scared rabbit darted back into the safety of her burrow, slamming the door behind her.

"Nice neighborhood you chose, Katherine." His voice was thickly coated with sarcasm. "Let me try that lock."

Katherine felt a hot flush invade her cheeks and her eyes were bright with shame. "You're not coming in," she told him, her desperation giving her words added emphasis.

"Don't try to stop me." He hissed the words as he took her arm and forcibly led her through the now open door.

"But you heard her. I'll lose my room."

"Doesn't look like much of a loss to me." Chad locked the door behind them and surveyed Katherine's austere apartment without favor while still dabbing at his cheek.

Katherine watched, her green eyes pleading. It was an agony to see him. The feelings he aroused in her cried out to be fulfilled, but Chad had made it clear that he was finished with her. What a fool he would think her to be if he should know of her secret longings. The only reason he had come, she told herself, was to see her humiliation.

She felt her knees weaken and edged her way to the armchair, sinking gratefully into its floral-printed cushions.

"You needn't have come," she told him. "I know I'm fired."

Chad eyed her with alarm. "Fired? What are you talking about?" He started for her, then stopped, his strong hands clenching into fists at his sides. "For pity's sake, Katherine, you're the last person we'd fire. In fact it's just the opposite. I'm here to tell you the job is yours. You were sensational today. What you did was nothing short of brilliant!"

Katherine looked up at Chad, feeling dazed. She wanted to believe him but it was all too much. She had the note; it was in her purse. Slowly she raised herself out of the chair. Her purse was by the door.

"Don't you understand?" Chad's voice was following her. "I've seen the photography. The China Line is a success. A smash success. You should hear how excited Joe is."

She had reached her purse and was searching its contents. "I've been fired, Chad, really I have." She handed him the slip of paper. "Eleanor did it and she still has the right to choose her office personnel." She swayed slightly. Her legs were still not strong. Cautiously she made her way back to the chair.

Chad studied the note and then her, his dark brows drawn together in a question. "This doesn't mean a thing." He crumpled the paper and dropped it on the table.

"Oh, yes, it does," Katherine insisted, but in a voice that was dragging with fatigue. "I never thought I'd say anything like this, but I've learned an awful lot in the few weeks I've been at Butler's. One thing is that no job is worth what went on today." She closed her burning eyes to hide the image of his face and continued, resigned to what must happen.

"I think I'd rather go home and get a job in the dry goods store than continue working for a person who would go to such lengths to preserve his own position."

Chad moved closer and lifted a limp hand. "Eleanor's the one who did the slashing."

"I know. She's the only one who could have done it, or who would want to." Katherine blinked her eyes and looked at him, perplexed. "How did you find out?"

"She told me, for one thing," he said easily as he seated himself on the arm of her chair and began toying with a tendril of her hair. "But that was at the end. In the beginning, when you found the damage, I had to make sure." His eyes roamed leisurely, caressing every inch of her body, and gradually a corner of his mouth began to curve in suggestion. "Remember last night, Katherine?"

The hint of intimacy in his voice alarmed her. Of course she remembered. The memory of last evening was seared on her soul like the brand of a fallen woman. Nervously she edged away from the danger of his nearness.

Chad laughed and rose from the chair. "No need to be so skittish, my pet." He walked over to her makeshift kitchen and inspected her meager facilities. "Want some coffee?"

She nodded. A hot, fragrant drink would be welcome. Chad filled her little kettle and turned on a burner.

"About last night," he said, returning to his theme. "That phone call I received." He paused and turned to her, his broad smile cutting a white swath across his tanned face and emphasizing the incredible magnetism of his virility. "I'm pretty sure I know who you thought was calling."

Katherine winced.

"But you're wrong. It was Dad." Again he paused to study her reaction. "Makes you feel better, does it? Good. Dad had flown in from Washington, not for today's photography as he told you, but because Eleanor's behavior had become intolerable. He wanted to talk. That's why I sent you home. You have to know it was not what I wanted to do."

Chad was smiling at the clear look of relief on Katherine's face. The kettle whistled fretfully and he returned to making their coffee. "Last night we spent hours discussing

178

the possibility of her being ill and what we should do about it." He glanced over his shoulder. "Cream? Sugar?"

Katherine shook her head. "No, thank you." She had suspected Eleanor's illness too, and looking back, the symptoms had been increasingly obvious.

Chad was stirring the steaming cups. "Today Eleanor's actions resolved any doubts we might have had. She's very ill, but not beyond recovery. When we asked her, she admitted what she had done and asked our help. You know Dad and his loyalty. He'll do everything he can for her." He lifted the cups and turned toward her, his eyes probing her intently. "The result is that Butler's is without a chief publicist—unless you want the job."

Katherine stared at him, speechless. An answer would not come. It had been enough to learn that he had not rejected her for Carole Seeley. But this question he posed was simply more than her tired and reeling mind could cope with.

"Don't you want it? Isn't it the answer to all of your ambitious dreams, Katherine Dunn?" His voice held a note of desperation.

She dropped her eyes to avoid him. Of course she wanted it—didn't she? A few weeks ago this chance was all that she longed for, but recently something new and much more important had entered her life, something that she could never deny again. And with that realization came the certainty that the "strictly business" relationship she had sought to have with Chad could never, ever appease the longings of her heart.

"How do you really feel about me?" Chad was demanding an answer in a voice that would brook no deception.

Katherine lifted a tearstained face, her green eyes dulled with misery. She could never tell him, he would only ridicule her.

"Is what Carole told me true?" He sounded almost incredulous.

"Carole?" Katherine gasped, horrified at what her conniving adversary might have said.

"You and she are not exactly the closest of friends, am I right?"

Katherine nodded unhappily.

"And she led you to believe that we—she and I—are lovers?"

"Yes!" The word exploded from her lips. "I thought—that is, she implied—you might be getting married."

"Oh, I am," he assured her blandly.

"What?" Katherine paled. "I thought you—"

"But not to Carole."

"Wh—wh—who?" Even her voice betrayed her trembling. She watched him, fearful of his answer. Chad put the cups back on the tiny drainboard and moved to Katherine, his expression smoky and mysterious.

"Isn't it time we put an end to our misunderstandings?" He was there before her, taking her hands, drawing her up, out of the chair, and into the closing circle of his arms.

"Do I actually matter to you as much as Butler's?" he murmured, kissing her throat.

"Oh, yes," she sighed. "More! Much, much more!"

Chad pulled his embrace tight and shuddered. "Katherine, Katherine, how I love you. That time I thought you were gone to the sea, I almost lost my mind."

"I was very foolish," she murmured. "But you did come for me—and I am so very glad that you did," she sighed at the memory.

"You rascal!" He kissed the top of her head. "Do you realize the consternation you caused me?"

Katherine shook her head blissfully.

"I wanted you," he whispered huskily. "And I took

you. Then afterward I felt terrible. I felt that I was guilty of using you in the most base way."

Katherine started to protest.

"No, darling. Let me finish. You see, I soon changed my mind. When I saw how eager you were to take over The China Line publicity I came to believe that you had traded that luscious body of yours for a chance at Eleanor's job. And that is why last night I was going to take you and not feel a twinge of remorse."

Katherine backed away from Chad's embrace.

"But none of that is true," she told him, her green eyes large with the fear that he would not believe her.

"I know that now."

His provocative smile appeared for an instant and then the wide, sensual mouth was hers, sweeping her up into a tide of feelings he had only given her glimpses of before. Katherine answered his every quest with a wanton pleasure, relishing the feel of his sensitive hands upon her body. His hungry need for her was growing insatiable and with it his hands, his lips, his whole being, became more and more demanding until, at last, he pulled himself away.

Katherine tugged at his arms, eager for him to press her close once more so that she could go on exploring the tingling variety of his kisses, but he held her away.

"Do you know what you have done for me?" His eyes were soft and filled with the vulnerability lovers offer one another. "After we lost Rob and Mom, I thought my heart was a stone. Everything pointed that way. Life seemed pointless, precarious, headed straight for death. And then, one day"—his lips curved into a tender smile of longing, and his eyes drifted over her with undisguised intimacy—"a leggy redhead fell at my feet and nearly snapped my head off when I tried to be a gentleman and help rather than be a beast and take advantage of her, as I was sorely tempted to do."

181

Katherine quivered in his arms, remembering the masterful caress of his hands upon her legs.

"From that moment I have had only one question growing in my mind, and now, my delicious redhead, you must answer it. Will you belong to me? Not just for this moment —but always?"

She nodded eagerly and reached out to draw him near. "I never could say no to you."

"I'm going to take you up on that, my darling, sweet, loving Kathy." He was kissing her eyelids. "My headstrong, officious Katherine." His lips were on her cheek and ear. "My sensuous, desirable Kate." He had reached her mouth and she was aching for the desire to give him all that she had held locked away for so long.

Tenderly, urgently, Katherine searched for his eyes and held them fast with her own. She had to tell him now, before they lost themselves completely in their need for one another. Slowly, from the hidden chambers of her heart, the words began to come.

"I love you, Chad . . . forever."

Katherine opened her eyes lazily and stretched beneath the coverlet like a well-satisfied cat.

What a wonderful dream that had been. But she thought, recalling her bedmate, no dream could begin to approach the glories of this reality.

Rolling over, Katherine surveyed with loving eyes the broad tanned back lying beside her. Chad's head was hidden beneath a pillow. Cautious not to wake him, she propped herself up on one elbow and lifted a corner of the pillow. The sight of Chad sleeping, his lashes spread like black fans upon his cheeks, brought a tender smile to Katherine's lips. Her husband looked so boylike, so vulnerable and innocent. From this view one would never guess that here was a man of thoughtful judgment, strong leadership, and infinite patience.

On the other hand, even with those magnetic dark eyes closed, the curve of his nostrils and the fine molding of his lips told of a fathomless well of passion. Here, too, was a man who cared, who felt, who took boldly what he wanted, and who loved completely. And he loved her!

183

My *husband!* Katherine exulted to herself as she sank back upon her own pillow and held her left hand up before her eyes. A large marquise diamond winked at her. But it was not the diamond that her eyes caressed. It was the wide gold band beneath it. The band, just like Chad's own, which proclaimed their love for one another, their mutual trust and fidelity . . . forever.

Looking beyond her hand, Katherine viewed the skylight overhead, one of the many small additions she and Chad had given Cielo together.

Fleecy clouds scudded across the pale sky. It was April. The days were still crisp, but the hills were green with new life.

What a wonderful time of year, she thought. All full of new beginnings. How appropriate if her private suspicions proved to be correct.

Katherine's "bride's year" was a full four months past. She was a thoroughly married woman now. How stupid she had been to think life could be complete any other way. She looked over at Chad's still form and whispered, "Thank you, darling, for saving me from myself."

A stray thought creased her forehead momentarily. If only her mother could have lived. She would have seen in Chad how good and kind and totally giving a man could be.

And her father? That was an unfinished page in her book. Chad was encouraging her to find him. He had offered to hire a firm to trace Jimmy Dunn, but Katherine held back. In some ways she was afraid to find him. What would he be like now? And what if he turned away from her again? Could she stand to be rejected a second time?

Again she turned her head on her pillow to gaze tenderly at her husband. Why should she be afraid of rejection? She had the whole world right next to her in this great big love-filled bed. Yes, she decided, today she would tell

Chad to hire that search firm and to tell them to hurry up with it. Because, as he had pointed out, Jimmy Dunn might well be more in need of his daughter than she had ever been in need of him.

Daughters. Fathers. Mothers. Sons. Familiar words that suddenly had new meanings for her. A stream of brand-new questions flooded her mind, and Katherine slid out of the bed to face herself in the long wall of mirrors.

Chad stirred but fell silent once again.

Looking good! She nodded at her reflection approvingly. The few pounds she had gained since marriage added nicely to the fullness of her breasts and the pleasant curve of her hips, while leaving her long legs trim and the line of her neck and shoulders soft but firm.

Yes, she acknowledged. It was impossible not to agree with the evidence of her own body presented. She was a woman in full flower, blooming with sensuality, health, and—she felt sure—that most miraculous blessing that only a woman could experience.

If she was right—and she was certain there could be no other explanation for these recent waves of queasiness or for the strange moments when she felt quite faint—there would be changes in her life. Changes in hers and Chad's lives that would be irrevocable. Would she mind? Smiling, she thought of Dee, pregnant for the second time, and of the boundless joy baby Peter had brought into her friend's life. No. She ran a hand over her still-flat stomach. No, how could she mind? On the shady side of twenty-five, she knew it was time for her to start a family. Oh, how she prayed that all of her children would be like Chad and Adam—and Lucy.

But what about Chad? How would he react when she told him of her suspicions? There might well come a time when their nights of lovemaking would be interrupted. A worried frown fled across her face. No, she shook herself.

That was a silly thing to worry about. Chad would not look for someone else to entertain him. He was hers as completely as she was his. They shared far more than their physical passion. They were one in spirit as well, working side by side in every venture from their business hours at Butler's to their hideaway at Cielo. And that was the way it would always be. Children would only add to the closeness they possessed.

"Hey!" Chad's voice rumbled from the bed. "Waking up to one Katherine Butler in the raw is enough to quicken any man." He was rolling off of the bed. "But two of you"—he pointed to the mirror—"is enough to drive me mad!"

In a bound he was behind her.

"I didn't mean to wake you up," she told him saucily.

"Well, you did."

His warm breath tickled her neck and his lips caressed her shoulders as his hands moved deliberately from her waist up to cradle her breasts and tease their rosy tips.

"Chad," she said, grasping his hands to stop their playfulness. "Will you love me even if I get fat?"

He laughed and tweaked her breasts again, sending a shock wave of desire rippling through her body.

"I'll love you no matter what. And I will love you the same way when you are a hundred and two, and when you are a thousand and two, and even when—"

Katherine managed to turn in his arms and place one hand gently against his lips.

"I think I'm pregnant," she said in a soft voice.

Chad stiffened and pursed his lips.

"You *think* you're pregnant?" he asked in a tone of voice that immediately resurrected all of Katherine's doubts and caused her green eyes to grow wide with apprehension.

"Hmm," he murmured and, lifting a finger, traced an

186

imaginary line from her lips, between her breasts, over her abdomen, stopping at her navel.

"Hmm," he murmured again.

"What does that mean?" Katherine demanded anxiously.

Smiling a secret smile, Chad swept her up into his arms and started back toward the bed.

"It means, my silly, desirable darling," he told her between kisses, "that I think I had better ensure the accuracy of your diagnosis."

When You Want A Little More Than Romance—

Try A Candlelight Ecstasy!

Wherever paperback books are sold!

Dell Bestsellers

- ☐ **NOBLE HOUSE** by James Clavell.............$5.95 (16483-4)
- ☐ **PAPER MONEY** by Adam Smith.................$3.95 (16891-0)
- ☐ **CATHEDRAL** by Nelson De Mille...............$3.95 (11620-1)
- ☐ **YANKEE** by Dana Fuller Ross.....................$3.50 (19841-0)
- ☐ **LOVE, DAD** by Evan Hunter.......................$3.95 (14998-3)
- ☐ **WILD WIND WESTWARD**
  by Vanessa Royal.....................................$3.50 (19363-X)
- ☐ **A PERFECT STRANGER**
  by Danielle Steel......................................$3.50 (17221-7)
- ☐ **FEED YOUR KIDS RIGHT**
  by Lendon Smith, M.D. $3.50 (12706-8)
- ☐ **THE FOUNDING**
  by Cynthia Harrod-Eagles..........................$3.50 (12677-0)
- ☐ **GOODBYE, DARKNESS**
  by William Manchester...............................$3.95 (13110-3)
- ☐ **GENESIS** by W.A. Harbinson.....................$3.50 (12832-3)
- ☐ **FAULT LINES** by James Carroll $3.50 (12436-0)
- ☐ **MORTAL FRIENDS** by James Carroll $3.95 (15790-0)
- ☐ **THE SOLID GOLD CIRCLE**
  by Sheila Schwartz $3.50 (18156-9)
- ☐ **AMERICAN CAESAR**
  by William Manchester...............................$4.50 (10424-6)

At your local bookstore or use this handy coupon for ordering:

Dell DELL BOOKS
P.O. BOX 1000, PINE BROOK, N.J. 07058-1000

Please send me the books I have checked above. I am enclosing $_____ (please add 75c per copy to cover postage and handling). Send check or money order—no cash or C.O.D.'s. Please allow up to 8 weeks for shipment.

Mr./Mrs./Miss_____

Address_____

City_____State/Zip_____